ISBN: 978-1-966037-57-6

2025 Encyclopocalypse Publications trade paperback edition.

BIG LIZARD

A NOVEL

JOE R. LANSDALE
KEITH LANSDALE

Encyclopocalypse Publications
www.encyclopocalypse.com

CONTENTS

BIG LIZARD

For the Bear.
Joe R. Lansdale

For Danni, my unicorn.
Keith Lansdale

FIVE YEARS AGO

FROM THE DAILY TIKTAALIK

COP CONSPIRACY OF HOMELESS HOMICIDES
Opinion piece by: Woody Burns

Officials continue to cover up details of yet another murdered destitute subject discovered last Friday night in the Tiktaalik downtown area.

When asked for official comment, police attributed the incident to violence among other vagrants, or possibly illegal immigrants, who live in the area. One member of the department commented off the record that, "It was a disturbance turned deadly due to an addiction to meth and a half-eaten ham sandwich."

Another officer said off the record, "Well, the ham sandwich might have been involved, but I suspect something more nefarious."

While officers on the case have been ordered not to comment on the matter officially, we here at *The Daily Tiktaalik* have been able to obtain photos of the scene, but due to their nature, cannot be printed in a public newspaper, but what we can state is it was a bloody crime scene and body parts were missing. A former FBI profiler who we contacted for the agent's experience and expertise, said the murders appear ritual, and match the other four bodies discovered this month. There was nothing to substantiate a quarrel over a ham sandwich. No sandwich appeared in the crime photos.

The Daily Tiktaalik has also obtained records from five years ago showing a matching five homeless subjects murdered in the same ritualistic manner.

There are multiple reports of similar murders occurring every five years dating back to the early nineteen hundreds. A time frame making it impossible for a single responsible party and instead the work of a possible cult. But why?

When the police were once again confronted with this information for comment, their only on record response was, "How do you keep getting in here?"

Why do authorities continue to hide the truth? What really led to their deaths? And was there ever a ham sandwich at all?

We here at *The Daily Tiktaalik* will continue to release more as this story develops.

THE PRESENT: BUSTER NIX

BUSTER NIX SHIFTED his plump butt in the cheap plastic chair, said, "So, you got something with a little more class than sexing chickens? I don't think that's for me."

The chair he was sitting in was uncomfortable, and it didn't help that his body wasn't that comfortable to begin with. Trick knees, a bad hip, and too much body weight made him feel more like a sack of potatoes than a man. He thought he might start a diet soon, maybe buy some barbells. Light ones. Have a salad for lunch. Maybe some chicken and mashed potatoes, and cut the dressing on the salad. Perhaps some honey mustard on it, once, maybe twice a week. Someone had suggested substituting tofu for meat in meals, but tofu tasted far too much like tofu, as far as Buster was concerned.

The Employment Office lady, squat and dark of skin with a blue bow in her hair, looking as if she had just swallowed a bug, said, "Did you say you want a job with class? You're looking for class, Buster, you need to have a college degree, maybe be part of the British royalty. A certificate from Barber College would be a step up for you. It's not like you've got a good track record."

"Ah, Auntie June. I don't have to be a brain surgeon. I just don't want something like last time."

"You got fired as a sign spinner. It was a gimmick sign, Buster. My cat could have done the job."

"Sign spinning is harder than it looks. I kept hitting myself in the mouth. And that cat of yours is pretty damn smart."

"Haha. Tiktaalik isn't a bustling metropolis, so even if you had some qualifications, there wouldn't be much available in the class area. Another thing, being black doesn't help."

"Not a lot I can do about that," Buster said. "And plus, we're both black."

"But I got a degree. You're black and unskilled and not likely to *be* skilled. Your hygiene's questionable, and hell, you dropped out of high school."

"Math's hard."

Buster stared at a poster mounted on the wall behind Auntie June. A cat was hanging on for dear life with the inspirational message of "Hang in there," printed at the top.

Buster wasn't sure why that was supposed to inspire him. That cat just looked fucked.

"Listen," Auntie June said, "They got a job at Sergeant's Pick-A-Chicken that isn't sexing the chickens. Night work."

"What kind of night work?"

"Security officer. You get a uniform, a flash- light and about fifty dollars a week to shake doors. I think some chicken meals go with the deal."

"That's it? Fifty dollars a week? I can't live off peanut butter sandwiches and buy a cardboard box to live in on that kind of money."

"You do all right for a few weeks, then you get bumped up to a more serious pay rate."

"How serious?"

"Not that serious, but it beats fifty bucks."

"That's it? All you got?"

Auntie June had a look on her face like someone who was used to disappointing people.

"Sorry, nephew. That's it."

"I carry a gun?"

"Chickens are pretty docile, Buster."

"Funny. All right. I'll take it. When can I start?"

"You got a drug test to do, pass that, you're in. Don't take any sleep medicine. It leaves a residue or some such."

"Just tell me where and when to pee."

THE PHONE WOKE BUSTER. He felt groggy. Not because it was too early, but because he slept a lot. Once the cable got shut off, there wasn't much else to do but sleep. What he needed was a solid job, a tooth filled, a massage, three weeks in the Bahamas, and a nice retirement package.

Buster reached from the couch to the ringing phone on the coffee table.

"Hello."

"Is that how you answer your phone?" It was his Aunt June.

"How am I supposed to answer it?"

"With enthusiasm."

"Okay. I'm enthused."

"Test came back clean. You start today."

"It's Sunday."

"It's three P.M. on Monday, Buster."

Buster picked up his large coke-bottle glasses and looked at the date on the clock to confirm.

"Jesus, Buster," she said. "You're a hot mess, boy. Weren't my sister's kid I swear. Shit, boy, find a clean shirt, brush your teeth, and don't be late. Matter of fact, brush your teeth twice. And don't wear the Batman socks."

IT WAS attempt number twelve to get little Trevor to sit down and eat. Buster knew his name because his mother had repeated it each of the twelve times, "Trevor, sit down and eat!"

Trevor stood up again, holding a nugget in his hand like a potential missile, and locked eyes with Buster in gunfighter fashion. Buster looked away, but when he looked back, there was Trevor, still holding the nugget in a threatening fashion.

Buster, attempting to disconnect from Trevor, looked around Sergeant's Pick-A-Chicken.

Behind the counter a young girl was taking orders at the register. She wore red and white checker board clothing to match the Pick-A-Chicken logo, with the most notable part of the outfit being the signature headwear, which looked like someone had taken a chicken, stuck their head up its ass and decided to call it a hat. Its rubbery head bobbed about as the workers moved.

A man who looked to be in his forties, maybe fifties, he had one of those faces that made it hard to tell, came out of the back. He was wearing the same outfit as the lady at the register.

He handed the cashier a few rolls of coins. It was the manager, Elroy Cuzzins. One of the last remaining relatives of the founder, Sergeant Cuzzins, whose recipe for chicken dated back to the Civil War. Buster recognized him from local TV ads next to pictures of the old Sergeant, both sporting the fowl head gear.

Buster wondered if the founder, Sergeant, had been the first one to wear the chicken hat. And if so, what were his real feelings about the headgear? By the look of the old Sergeant, he looked like a man that might have felt comfortable wearing a live chicken.

Elroy spotted Buster sitting in the booth and waved him

over. Buster got up as spryly as he could, trying to look every round inch like a security guard, and look enthused.

"Mr. Nix?" Elroy said, as Buster reached across the counter and shook his hand.

"Just call me Buster."

"Buster then. I apologize for being a little late, something I try not to be. But I had a chicken matter to attend to, and it couldn't wait. Ready for the baby chicken tour, Buster."

"The what?"

Elroy pushed open a low gate to let Buster behind the counter.

"We call it that instead of the two-bit tour. Someone in management thought it was clever and, you know, small tour, small chicken."

"Someone in management?"

"Yeah. Me."

"Nice," Buster said, and wormed a smile across his face. He decided that Elroy most likely loved that chicken hat with a passion. Likely didn't even take it off when he got home, kicking back in the La-Z-Boy, the news on TV, a beer in hand.

Elroy led Buster toward the rear of the restaurant, and through a door that led outside and into the fenced Picking Yard.

"The idea came from seafood places," Elroy said. "The good ones let you pick your own lobster, sometimes your own fish. So, why not pick your own chicken?"

They moved around the lot and through a mass of live clucking chickens. Other diners were there as well, eyeballing possible selections. They had on yellow rain slickers with hoods.

"Way we see it, you just want to order chicken, you're fixed up, but if you like the idea of picking your own, having us butcher it, we can do that. We also have, for a slightly larger fee, a program where you can pick your own, kill it, clean it, dip it in our specially prepared batter, and put it in the deep fryer. Our cooks manage quality control, of course."

"Do many people actually pick a chicken and kill it and so on?"

"They do, indeed. Children, of course, must be accompanied by an adult. When they brandish the hatchet to chop off the chicken's head, we like to think they have adult supervision, which not only helps them and others avoid injury, the blood is more likely to go into the trough. That's the trough right over there."

Elroy pointed this out as if Buster couldn't see it, but even with his bad eyesight and old prescription glasses, he could see it clearly.

"You put their heads on that block, chop away, and the blood spurts out of their necks into the trough. It can still be imperfect and messy, that's why we provide those chicken-foot-yellow rain-coats"

"Many injuries?"

"A little retarded kid lost a toe once. Should never have been given an axe, and I mean that kindly. She couldn't help that she didn't have no sense. It would be like giving you a jet to fly, minus the instructions."

"Interesting way of looking at it," Buster said.

There were several people at the chopping block. Axes went up, axes went down, blood spurted into the trough and all about it like water from a fire hose. Sometimes it took a couple of chops to subdue lunch. The yard was filled with a lot of squawking, injured chickens and laughing children. A few headless chickens had gotten loose of their consumers and were racing around the yard before collapsing in a heap of quivering feathers. One of the headless chickens wasn't a quitter, and was being chased by a fat kid in orange sneakers. He was giggling and trying to strike the dead but mobile chicken with his hatchet. Buster was surprised it wasn't little Trevor.

Elroy said, "Thus the saying, like a chicken with its head cut off."

The dead chicken finally collapsed, and the boy in the orange sneakers chopped at it with enthusiasm until his father came and took the axe away.

"That's a chicken that won't be eaten today. Hacked much too badly. But it happens now and then."

Buster thought Pick-A-Chicken wasn't so much an exclusive fast food restaurant, as it was a breeding ground for potential serial killers.

"I get the idea," Buster said, hoping to curtail the chicken yard visit.

"And here's something you'll like," Elroy said. "Long as you're a part of the Sergeant Pick-A-Chicken family, you can choose a chicken once a day for your very own Cluster Cluck Meal. Or you can just order a meal without harvesting it yourself."

Harvesting. Hunters used that word too, instead of kill. Buster thought you ought to call a thing what it was, and not put a coat and tie on it. The word was kill. But Buster, thinking of the rent, said, "Thanks for that."

"Just know that biscuits cost extra. They're big, though, so they're worth the price, and there's a ten percent discount, with coupon."

"You need a coupon if you work here?"

"You do. Check the newspaper on Wednesdays."

Elroy led Buster out of the yard and into a larger enclosure surrounded by a tall chain link fence with a gate at the rear. There were metal curlicue chickens in the fence work. There were a number of enormous buildings at the back of the place, and in some of the buildings large windows were filled with mammoth fans. You could hear the fan blades beating the air about like a dominatrix spanking a banker's ass.

"Those buildings are where the chickens are kept. You

could land a jumbo jet in those suckers. Out back of them, that's where the chickens are sexed, and beyond that, for those that prefer not to pick their chicken or butcher it, there's the butcher shop where they prepare the Basic Cluster Cluck Combos. Cut up and ready to fry. Dad always said those were the best meals, cheap and simple. But I got to tell you, those cardboard boxes they go into, that's where the real money adds up. I'm thinking of a bring your own box deal of some sort. Still working on it. Nothing set in stone yet."

Elroy pointed. "Over there's a few storage buildings. Need to check the locks, maybe the insides once or twice a week, but the one on the far end, with the padlock about the size of my head, the big red building, you needn't worry about that. We don't use that one. Well, sometimes we do. Just private business. Keeping our quality up and staying on top. We believe you have to do what needs to be done to stay on top, and that means screwing over our competition with better ideas and better prices."

Elroy's pleasant expression turned sour, as if a shitty memory had surfaced like a corpse in the well.

Buster watched Elroy's expression gradually turn back to something more managerial.

"Here now, let me show you your shack, as we call it."

They made their way to a decent sized aluminum building with a smaller fan similar to the ones in the chicken housing. Elroy used an old-fashioned key on a ring of keys to open the door.

Inside, Elroy waved his hand around, said, "Right in here, you got your work space. Computer for filing reports, your vouchers for your week's pay. Don't need to really worry about that, long as you punch the time card in the restaurant kitchen. Sometimes there's overtime. We sell until midnight every night. Another way we stay ahead of the competition. Be surprised how many people want a Cluster-Cluck for a late-night snack. Keep that ass fat is our unofficial motto. Very unofficial. Forget I said that. I should mention, that after the toilet paper runs out, you got to provide your own. Ass wiping adds up to money. Anyway, you're here from midnight until we open at nine in the morning for eggs and chicken breakfast sandwiches. You punch out then."

"Aren't I just getting paid for eight hours?"

"You are, but you have a supper break, and that's an hour, we figure a few fifteen-minute breaks during the night for coffee, whacking off in the back room, whatever, and we're lucky to get six hours from you. Remember, dinner break you check out the time card, check back in when you finish. And do be on time. You have an hour exactly to eat. This job, you mostly walk around and pull doors and wait until morning. Things go sideways for some reason, someone trying to get in and mess with the chickens, we need to know and put a stop to it. We've had a few sexcapades in the past, you know. Good thing a guard was on duty."

"Sexcapades?"

"Guys slipping in to noodle the chickens."

"That's a thing?"

"It was *their* thing. Guess, guys like that, they've got experience down on the farm, busted a few eggs in their time, and they want to keep their hand in. Or rather their dick."

"Wow," Buster said.

"Yeah. Got to keep an eye out. And then there's just the plain ole chicken nabber. Some homeless Mexican might come in and steal a chicken to cook, or you got your vandals, just messing things up because they can. You're here to prevent that. Might want to get yourself a nightstick or something. You don't look like much of a tumbler. Anyway, you got a lot of free time, but it's a big responsibility. We close on Christmas and after two P.M. on Thanksgiving—be surprised how many people buy chicken those days. Martin Luther King Day is optional, so sometimes we have a short day, you know, short staffed. You would work those days, though. Bottom line, Buddy—"

"Buster."

"Buster. Bottom line is make sure doors are locked, no one is fucking or stealing the chickens, and you can snooze on the couch a bit, for all I care. But just a bit. Regular rounds are necessary along with a certain alertness."

"Of course."

"Just stay out of the Red House, as I like to call it. That's off limits. I told you that, though, didn't I?"

"You did."

"Well," Elroy poked out his hand, and Buster shook. "Welcome to the Sergeant Pick-A-Chicken family. Everyone here is family including Miss Journey, the main cook, and she's hard to live with sometimes."

THE LINE WASN'T MOVING. Buster hung his arm out the window of his '93 Honda Civic as he waited in the drive-through for his free Cluster Cluck meal. He'd decided to pass on any extra biscuits, being they were still an unnecessary luxury he couldn't afford, and he had yet to acquire coupons.

Two weeks of guarding chickens hadn't been that bad, and while he waited on his order, he contemplated the job so far. It was mostly just a lot of sitting around. Watching the clock and finding fun little ways of passing the time. His favorite activity so far had been naming some of the chickens in the pick lot, and sometimes giving them back stories. Their stories ended quite abruptly once they were chosen. It all began to feel like murder to Buster. Here he had made up a back story for a hen from Cacciatore, and the next thing you knew, it was having its head chopped off with an axe.

Most of the chickens looked pretty much the same. They pecked at the dirt and ran into each other like little chicken bumper cars, knocking one another about and then hurriedly running away like they had somewhere to be. Possibly late to the fryer.

One night on his rounds, he'd decided to sit for a moment to rest his bad hip. After sitting down on a low bench in the chicken yard, he realized he had made a mistake, as getting up was more than he could easily manage.

As he searched for the strength to stand, a little white chicken broke from the fowl sea of white chickens and came over to nestle against Buster.

Unlike most of the chickens bouncing around, her talons were mostly white, and Buster appropriately named her Socks.

Buster told Socks everything that night. About his past relationships, and how they'd gone to shit for every reason but his own fault. His back troubles. His knee troubles. His bill troubles. Hell, he even talked politics. And Socks was a great listener. She sat and almost looked to be nodding in agreement, like she understood not only what was said, but the great mysteries of the universe.

The next night, Buster went back to locate Socks again, but she wasn't anywhere to be found. The chicken picking yard was wall-to-wall with fowl, so she might have just gotten lost in the pile, but Buster feared Socks might have gone on to that great deep fryer in the sky.

At the drive-through window, he presented his employee ID. He didn't have the clout to get it Clucked Up, which meant an extra chicken leg and coleslaw would be added, but he felt that worked to his advantage. He needed to lose a few pounds. More than a few. They gave him his Cluster Cluck Meal and off he went.

He decided to go a few blocks down the road to find a place to park and eat, but that turned into a trip to the outskirts of town where old abandoned warehouses and former business buildings were. They were up on a hill, and he could see the lights of the town from there. It was close, yet so far away.

Buster pulled into the parking lot of one of the abandoned crumbling buildings. It was kind of sad, but it felt better than sitting in a restaurant alone. When he did that, he felt people could sense his loneliness, the way predators could sense a wounded animal, and that just made him feel worse.

Buster threw the car in park, killed the lights, and opened his box. A couple of deep-fried pieces of chicken, a single biscuit, and two packets of Creamy Cluck Sauce. The free meal didn't include sides, which was a shame because the only time Buster's diet ever got close to a vegetable was when it was deep fried.

Buster took a bite of chicken, and then wondered if maybe he was eating his only friend, Socks. He had no plans of becoming a vegetarian, but the thought unnerved him, like maybe an accidental cannibal's feast of a cousin might put them off a barbecued rib, at least for a weekend.

Buster decided to eat just the biscuit. He wasn't sure what Creamy Cluck Sauce was, but there were two packets of it in chicken shaped plastic containers. Did it go on the biscuit or the chicken? He couldn't figure it, and decided to pass. The biscuit tasted as if it had been left in the pocket of a suit coat that had been dry-cleaned. He was glad he didn't have to pay for it. Elroy's comments on the deliciousness of the biscuits was highly overrated.

He glanced about as he nibbled his biscuit. There was paint graffiti sprayed on the brick walls. One of the bits of information was in tall white letters. It read: "For a good time, call Brenda." There was also a phone number.

Buster thought for a moment, then took a pad from the glove box and wrote the name and number down, then tore the page out, wadded it up and threw it on the floorboard.

Jesus, what had he come to?

As Buster's eyes became better adjusted to the dark, he realized that the building he was parked in front of was shaped like a boat made of bricks; he could make out its outline in the moonlight. It was huge. There was a row of round porthole windows along the sides of the wall, spread out about every six feet.

There was a wad of vines and moss all along the top of the brick wall, and there were trees growing up against it. In a gap between vines, moss and trees, was a weathered sign. The sign bore a painting of a robed man with a long white beard, holding a crooked staff. A sheep was at his feet, eating grass. There was a look on the bearded man's face like something cold had just been shoved up his butt. There was a frilled graying white banner painted above his head, and on it, stenciled big were the words, "Noah's Creationist Museum and Gift Emporium."

A smaller sign at Noah's feet read: "Not Open Sundays."

Buster remembered the place now. It had been built by an eccentric millionaire, had animatronics of animals and humans inside. He read about the Christian theme park in the newspaper. The park had lasted almost six months, then gone out of business, subject to a lack of dedicated creationists and a problem with a bucking dinosaur or some such. Lawsuits were filed. The millionaire had gone into the edible panty business, and from what Buster understood, he was doing quite well there. The panties came in a variety of colors and flavors and could be stretched to fit any ass. Choose strawberry, add your own chocolate skid stains, and you were ready for lunch or dinner, or your partner was.

As Buster took in the grand scope of the structure, there was movement behind one of the portholes.

A young, dark face was looking out at him.

Buster stared back at the figure, wondering if it was just his imagination. Maybe a poster, or one of the old animatronics that looked real.

Then it vanished, leaving only an empty porthole.

Buster kept watching, wondering if the face would return, when a loud knocking startled him so much, he jerked, sending the partially-eaten biscuit into the backseat.

He looked out the driver's window to see a black man with a large hat and droopy brown overcoat, leaning against the glass. The man had what looked like a spoiled cucumber for a nose. If the guy was here to rob him, he was about to be disappointed.

"Hey," the man said.

Buster rolled down the window a few inches. "Can I help you," Buster said.

The man pointed at the chicken in the box. "You gonna eat that chicken? I seen you sitting there with it, and wondered."

Buster looked at the box that may or may not have been Socks.

"You know what?" Buster said, rolling down the window, poking the box out at him. "It's yours."

"Thank you, sir," the man said, and took the box.

"You came up really silent like."

"You was mentally involved. I get like that sometimes, you know, thinking on a problem, and when I'm in that place, shit, you could drive a dump truck up my ass and I wouldn't notice it."

"You know it's like ninety degrees," Buster said. "Coat seems hot."

"You get used to it. Easier to keep up with if you wear it all the time. Thanks for the chicken. Is there a biscuit with it?"

"Not anymore. I'd stay away from the Creamy Cluck Sauce, though. Just guessing on that, but it's my suggestion."

"Gotcha," the man said, touching his fingers to his forehead in salute, and then he ambled away.

Buster checked his watch. So much for dinner.

Time to punch in.

⬇

AT THE LOT, Buster unlocked the gate, drove inside, locked it up again, parked, punched the time card in the kitchen. He was back on the clock. He limped to his shack and had a glass of orange juice, then picked up his flashlight and began wandering the perimeter. He walked by the chicken yard, leaned forward and looked through the fence. He didn't see Socks. He was probably being digested at this very moment, or being shit down the toilet, or if the guy he gave the box to ended up with Socks as his meal, shit out behind a bush somewhere.

Buster waddled about, favoring his knees. He unlocked doors and prowled around inside with his flashlight. One building was all freezers, stocked with ready-to-go butchered chickens. He opened one of the freezers and looked inside. The chickens were wrapped in clear plastic.

He moved on, shone the light in dark corners. Only shadows.

Outside, he locked the doors again and shook them to make sure they were well secured, and finally he came to the building in the back of the lot, the Red House, that Elroy said should be left alone, as far as inside examination went.

Buster decided he should check the lock, though, just to be thorough.

He shook the door gently. It was secure. He was about to walk away when he heard a noise inside. At first, he thought it was singing, but then he recognized it as something different entirely.

Someone, more than one someone, was chanting.

Buster slipped his key into the lock, and tried to open the door as silently as possible. He decided not to turn on his flashlight, as there was a glow at the far end of the tiled corridor, spilling out of the open doorway.

Buster clutched the flashlight like the club he hadn't wanted, and eased in that direction.

The chanting grew louder. Buster tracked close to the wall, came to the open door and looked inside.

The room was filled with an orangish light. It came from braziers positioned around a large pentagram in the center of the room, and sitting akimbo at the edges of the pentagram were a number of robed figures. The robes were a dark blue with white chicken designs on them. The chickens appeared to be dancing. The robes had hoods, and the hoods were a version of the chicken heads the employees wore, red wattles at the top.

There was a crate with several chickens in it. One of them was Socks. Buster could see her white feet clearly in the light of the coal-fed braziers. So, this was where she had ended up.

The chanting reached a crescendo, and then one of the hooded figures stood up, and from that new angle, Buster could see it was none other than Elroy. His face was painted with the light and there were beads of sweat on his forehead, and they appeared in the strange glow like little blisters. He was holding open a big fat, leathery book bound with metal bands.

"Now, we come to you again for another five years in the business, and we bring you our sacrifices, and the promise of other souls other than these chickens, which seems fair enough for all that you grant us, great Lizard Lord. Enjoy your small sacrifices with greater sacrifices to come in return for success."

It was then one of the men opened the crate and pulled out one of the chickens, and quicker than could be imagined, produced a short-curved knife and cut its throat. Blood sprayed into the pentagram, and Buster saw that the pentagram was etched deep into the floor, not drawn on it. The blood from the sacrificed chicken began to run into the runnels that made up the pentagram design. Buster eased forward slightly, mesmerized and horrified at the same time.

He could see that in the center of the pentagram was the design of a big lizard biting the head off a chicken. There was another design of a large bag at the lizard's feet, and a man was reaching out of the bag, his head, extended arm, and upper torso, visible. He seemed to be pleading pointlessly with the large chicken-eating lizard. The designs were crudely shaped. A child with only fundamental talent could have drawn them.

As the blood ran, flowing through the design, coming to rest where the lizard shape was, the first chicken was tossed onto the pentagram. With practiced professionalism, the man reached into the crate, and a second chicken was yanked out.

Buster was relieved to see that Socks, perhaps aware of what was going on, as much as chickens are aware, had moved to the back of the crate.

The fresh chicken's throat was cut, held in such a way that the blood sprayed onto the pentagram, into the little design gutters, same as before. The brazier's light changed color, flickered a poisonous green. In the center of the penta-gram, right where the lizard design was, there was a flutter of shadow, and the shadow turned as green as the light from the braziers, then it began to take shape. A green shadow in the form of a crouched lizard.

Elroy lifted his hands and bowed his head as the other man held the chicken to bleed out.

"We call upon you Lizard Lord, and appreciate your trip from the demonic world, and we offer you seven days of freedom from your confines, as well as five greater sacrifices than these, in return for good flocks of chickens and dollars in the coffer, and if it wouldn't hurt you none, about two more inches for all our dicks."

Elroy's assistant tossed the dead chicken into the penta-gram, pulled another from the crate, cut its throat with the same quick assurance as the other two.

The green shadow lifted its head, showed its teeth, white as a fresh snowball. All Buster could think in that moment was Socks was next. He knew whatever was going on wasn't exactly common, but what he wanted right then was to rescue Socks. It was the closest thing he had to a friend, and he wasn't about to let her die because of some crazy assholes in chicken-themed robes and hoods.

He made his way forward, and that's when his bad knee betrayed him. He stumbled against one of the braziers, knocking it over, sending flaming green, fiery coals into the pentagram. Something about that connection caused the interior of the pentagram to light up like the big night at Burning Man, and suddenly the green, wispy shape of the lizard turned its head in Buster's direction.

There was some kind of odd connection then. Buster felt something move in the back of his brain, like a large, venomous snake trying to lie down on his conscience. Then the pentagram became brighter, and there was an explosion that knocked Buster winding, but not before he saw the lizard's shadow advancing rapidly toward him. He saw too the big leather book go flying, and words, or more precisely pictographs, flipped from the pages, flew free of it like little white insects.

Elroy was bathed in green light and chicken feathers from the fresh kills, and the white shapes from the book covered him and they bathed Buster too; they lit on him buzzing and biting, buried up in his skin like tumors.

Socks could have moved to Cuba for all Buster cared at that point. He was more concerned with the fact that he was suddenly on fire and the pain was so intense he dove down into unconsciousness, amidst those licking emerald flames, flying chicken feathers, and swirling hieroglyphics, hoping to find cool comfort there.

WHEN BUSTER AWOKE he could smell bacon, and a fainter aroma of disinfectant. He hurt so bad it felt as if someone were pulling his innards out through his throat with a hot garden rake. Someone was screaming as well, really loud. It was so annoying Buster felt as if his bones were grating together.

And then there was a lot of white, and then the white became more of a soft buttery yellow glow, and Buster found himself awake.

In that moment, he learned several things. He was the one that smelled like bacon, and the annoying scream was coming from him.

"He needs more morphine," he heard his aunt say, and moments later he felt a lot less pain, and then no pain, and finally he seemed to be floating on a cloud and the cloud was cool and soft as a mama's touch. His pain had gone. He had a memory of green flames and noise, a large lizard, and chicken feathers, and finally he remembered lying outside the building on a strip of concrete with one leg twisted awkwardly up under him, and blazing nearby was the building with the pentagram, and the rest of the buildings, including the flagship restaurant, and all the chickens, were on fire too. He was just raw, hot meat lying on a concrete slab with charred chicken feathers floating above him. After that, all he remembered was now, and now was pretty good. The morphine was good. It was the best thing in the world, or for that matter, all the cosmos. He lay there and observed flaming chickens, dancing.

His aunt leaned over him. "Buster. Are you all right?"

"How much of me is left?"

"You're mostly there, but they had to set your leg and put in some metal rods and pins and sew up a gap in your testicles."

"Oh, hell."

"It was just a couple inches long."

"Double hell."

"And you're missing a toe," she said. "Not an important one."

"They all felt pretty important."

"The worst part is the burns."

"Tell me about it. Can you see chickens on fire, dancing?"

"I can see you."

"I feel like I'm all wrapped up, like a mummy." "Because you are. You're swathed in bandages

and salve from head to toe."

"How... do I look?"

"I can see your eyes. They look okay, little red where they should be white, smoky around the edges. It's bad."

"Don't spare me."

"Okay. It's really bad."

"Shit. Lie to me."

"You look fine."

"Damn it, Auntie June. You never knew how to comfort anyone."

"I know. Doctor says when you get healed, and it'll take a while, you'll be fine. 'Cept the toe. Might need a whole lot of skin grafts, bone replacement. You'll look different. Might need a new driver's license photo. And by the way, your car got blown up as well."

"First few days on the job, and it's turned out swell."

He felt his eyelids sag. "Sleep," said his aunt.

"Man, that stuff they gave me is some kind of shit, I tell you. I feel so good I want to get out of bed."

"I wouldn't," Aunt June said.

Then the morphine took him farther away, and his soft,

white cloud grew dark and swelled up around him and swallowed him, and carried him down into the deep dark.

And unbeknownst to him, something strange shifted inside of him. Bones rustled. Organs shifted. Blood pumped vigorously. His flesh quivered like jelly.

ALL GOOD THINGS come to an end.

The pain set in so hard and fast, it caused Buster to jar awake, certain that someone was holding a hot frying pan against his forehead.

His vision blurred from the pain, as if he was looking through Vaseline smeared over imperfect lenses. Looming over him was a figure, tall and dark, its mouth opening and closing, lips smacking, wet with saliva.

The pain bounced from his head and worked its way south. His vision cleared and the figure took shape, forming a thin man with a triangular face and a mustache, those saliva-damp lips. The man was holding a manila envelope. He realized the man was talking.

Ignoring him, Buster said, "Can you turn the drugs back on?"

The man dropped the envelope on the bed, next to Buster, and the sharp corner catching his burnt thigh might as well have been a dueling wound, sending more jolts of pain bouncing around inside his body.

Buster tried to sit up, but failed. He was in too much pain and the bandages limited his movements.

"Are you the devil?" Buster asked.

"The devil?" the man said. "Not quite. My name is William Whiner, and I'm the legal counsel for Sergeant-Pick-A-Chicken, and Sergeant-Pick-A-Chicken, Inc."

"Do they make you say the whole thing every time?"

"I am here on behalf of the Sergeant line to inform you

that while you were an employee of the company, you had not passed the probation period, and thus, you are not carried by our insurance."

"Great," Buster said. "Can you call a nurse on your way out? I need morphine."

"Medical staff can tell you this when they return, but here's a preview. They advised me that without insurance, they won't be able to supply you with any further assistance."

"Are you serious?" Buster said. "I'm about to pass out from pain."

"My advice, sleep is free. It might be your best bet."

"Well thank you for that Mr. Weiner."

"It's Whiner."

"Whatever."

"To cover the cost of the damages to the facility, the cost of the poultry, the funeral arrangements and personal family lawsuits of those who died in the explosion, though Elroy's body hasn't been discovered and is missing and assumed dead, not to mention a grease fire that spread to the Kroger warehouse next door, your bill, as far as we've deduced it at the moment, before your own medical expenses and a possible and ambitious lawsuit from Kroger, is upwards of eight-point-three million dollars and some change."

"Guess not knowing the change doesn't really alter anything, does it?"

"Probably not."

"Why am I to blame?"

"You survived. Someone has to be blamed."

"And when I can't pay?"

"Well, there's some good news on that side."

"I could use some."

"Likely some jail time in your future following the arson investigation. Free room and board, though. And there's the exercise yard."

"Try to fall down the elevator shaft on your way out."

"Who knows?" Whiner said. "Maybe you'll meet some interesting people and make some lasting friendships."

Buster wasn't sure what made him pass out again, but assumed it was a toss-up between another sharp wave of pain or the news of his forthcoming incarceration. At least prison food couldn't be any worse than here.

IN THE MIDDLE of the night, the twisting of his tail brought Buster awake.

A nurse had come in earlier with his clothes in a bag and told him he could finish out the night, but tomorrow morning it was a wheelchair ride to the curb.

But now, there was the large, green tail, and that was hard to figure. It was thrashing around between his legs.

And there were memories coming hotter and faster than before, the whole séance thing he'd witnessed. He was sure now that it had been real. What was up with that?

Maybe the drug had given him false memories and visions. That seemed the obvious conclusion. He considered on ways to make eight million dollars and some change for a while, but the best he could come up with was a lemonade stand. That method would take some time.

He lay there looking at the tail wave between his legs. Big and fat, long and dark green. It had broken open the bandages that swathed his butt and had pulled loose his catheter and colostomy bag.

He felt as if someone were pumping his insides full of air, like a great fart was about to awaken. And then the wrappings on his body began to snap. He flexed his fingers, digging into the sheets, felt them tear deep into the mattress. He lifted his hands before his face. Green hands and long black claws from which the innards of the sheet and mattress dangled.

He thought, now that's some shit. Perhaps it was an allergic reaction to the drug.

He realized another thing. He didn't hurt anymore. He felt strong and powerful. He also felt longer and heavier. His head was pressed against the wall behind the bed, and his enormous feet were dangling off the end of the mattress. One of his toes was missing.

He used the little device on his bed to raise himself. He rolled out of bed and made his way to the bathroom, turned on the light. He looked in the mirror and let out a short scream.

He was, like, well, he didn't know. Some kind of fucking alligator, with scales, and there was enough of him to make a couple good-sized suitcases, a wallet, a change purse and at least one shoe.

Most of the hospital gown he had worn had been torn by his growth. He realized too he resembled the lizard creature he had seen in the pentagram. The one that caught on fire and exploded, though he felt he had a friendlier face.

He looked in the mirror again, opened his snout. It was filled with some nasty looking teeth. He leaned forward, bumped his "nose" on the mirror. He was amazed to discover he had yellow eyes, and his business was hanging out of his ripped gown.

At least he had that going for him. Whatever was happening here had given him an impressive green pecker. Elroy had wished for two inches, well, he had topped out Elroy's wish. Hell, had that wish been given to him by accident?

Staggering out of the bathroom, mindlessly moving back to his bed, a nurse came into the room. She was carrying a chart. She was cute and wore a crisp outfit and a matching little white hat.

They stood and looked at one another.

Buster, being a gentleman, used his hands to unsuccessfully shield his new equipment, and said, "Hello."

At least his voice sounded like him.

He didn't know a person could jump three feet straight up, change direction in midair, and rush out the door, but she did. It was impressive.

Buster heard her screaming in the hallway. She had some lungs. She kept yelling "There's a monster in Room 34B."

That would be him.

Buster concluded that his being a lizard in a hospital room wouldn't work out for the best. He imagined cops, revolvers, a warning shot in the back of the head, and if not that, maybe zoo time.

Buster scurried to the large window. Damn. He could scurry fast, suddenly, and painlessly. He slid back the curtains. The window wasn't the sort that opened, as far as he could tell. He punched through it, listened as broken glass tinkled down the side of the building and onto the parking lot below.

Buster leaned out of the window, and as he heard a commotion in the hall, he put a foot on the sill, and stepped out of the fourth-floor and onto the window ledge, reached back, and delicately closed the curtains.

It was breezy on the ledge and the air was full of the smell of the nearby Dairy Bob; hamburgers, French fries, the sweet aroma of aging grease.

Peering at the ground below him, Buster saw an older black lady with a walker wearing a large church hat and a shawl. She was slowly making her way from her car to the emergency entrance of the hospital. She wasn't fast, but she was determined.

She didn't look up.

He considered his choices; shuffle left or shuffle right. Neither looked any better than the other. The noises from the hall had moved into his room. He knew he needed to decide quickly.

It was at that moment Buster learned the window did in fact swing open. Someone inside pushed the broken window frame out, and the frame caught him under the tail, and he was airborne.

His tail reflexively slashed out and began to spin, like a helicopter trying to fly. For all the good it was doing, he might as well have had a white surrender flag fastened to it.

Buster spun completely around, clawed at the wall, trying to gain real estate. He clutched at the second-floor ledge, but a large chunk broke loose in his hands. Down he went, concrete dust and ledge fragments raining around him.

He hit the ground, hard, falling behind a clutch of shrubbery.

The lady with the large hat, wheezing and clanking her way to the door, turned toward the noise of Buster's fall.

With shaky insistence, she used the walker to change course, made her way to the bush.

"Are you okay, young man?" she said.

Buster looked down, saw he'd turned back into himself; black and chubby, no tail. But on the plus side, there were no longer any burns. He was merely scratched up and his tail bone hurt. He was still missing a toe.

The old lady didn't even flinch at the sight of his little lizard, which had also changed back. He missed the lizard one already.

"Peachy. Just doing a bit of night gardening."

"Without no clothes?"

"Makes me feel closer to nature and I don't get my pants dirty."

"That's thinking ahead, I guess. But maybe you ought to take this." She peeled the shawl around her neck off and flipped it to him.

The old lady shrugged, and returned on her mission.

WITH THE SHAWL wrapped around his waist, Buster made his way to the creek behind the hospital. There was an animal trail alongside the water that went in the direction of his apartment.

He was deeply confused. Had he really turned into a lizard, and if so, why had he turned back? Maybe it had just been an imaginary side effect of the drugs. Or the pain. Maybe both. And yet, he was no longer burned and his knees didn't hurt. He hadn't felt this good since he was a kid. What the hell was going on?

No answers presented themselves.

It took a little more than an hour, and he had only been frightened twice, once by a raccoon, and another time by a stray dog drinking water from the creek. Both times he felt a swelling inside himself, and thought for a moment, he was transforming again. He felt that way every time he was startled or stressed, and tonight, that was often.

By the time he reached the area where his apartment was, his feet were cut and bloodied and he decided the lizard event had to have been due to the séance and explosion. Nothing else made sense. In fact, that didn't make a lot of sense either, but it was the best explanation he had. Except for drug hallucinations. He was hanging on to that idea for general comfort, but it was losing ground. A hallucination didn't cure burns.

Easing out of the creek bed, Buster rushed toward the door of his apartment, which was fortunately on the lower floor. There was a single light on above the door, the one he always left on when he went to work. Bugs buzzed around it like a halo.

He realized he didn't have his key, and then he saw it didn't matter.

There was an eviction noticed taped to the door.

He had been in the hospital so long his rent had come due, and his landlord, who was without patience, had evicted him. His heart sank like the Titanic.

He leaned against the door, feeling defeated, glanced to the curb. There was a row of trashcans there, green ones on little wheels. Hanging out of one of them was his stuffed monkey, Kala, that his aunt had given him when he was a boy. It clung to the side of the can by one arm.

Buster limped to the curb, his feet sore and stiff. He looked in the cans. His clothes were in one. His PlayStation was in the other, along with his game collection. There were black plastic bags in the other cans, most likely filled with his meager treasures.

Sighing deep, Buster pulled clothes from one of the cans, picked a wardrobe. Put on a shirt, pants, socks and shoes. He didn't locate his underwear right away. He found those after he was dressed. He stuffed a few items into the rolling trash can with the clothes he decided to keep, then pulling his monkey from the lip of the other trash can, he draped it around his neck, taking in the pleasant aroma of cinnamon and vanilla, as well as something less aromatic from the trashcan.

He stuck his PlayStation and games into the rolling trash-can, added a few choice items, and then, absent of a plan, began to push it toward the road, but hesitated. There was a bike path near that area of the creek, and he went that way, pushing the wheeled trashcan in front of him, making good time going nowhere.

THE MOON LOOKED ragged due to thin clouds tracing across it, and the night trail along the creek was full of the smell of the water and dead fish, and there was the sounds of crickets and frogs in the air.

After pushing the can aimlessly for an hour or so, the bike trail played out and there was a barrier of trees. Buster stopped and took in a deep breath, fought back tears. Emotionally he felt as if he had been dropped off a cliff.

He leaned against the can and had a good cry. When he finished, he looked up. There was a split in the trees, and he could see just beyond the split that there was a wall, and there was white writing on the wall that read, "For a good time, call Brenda," and then a phone number.

He knew where he was. He pushed through the gap in the trees as the thin clouds cleared before the moon and the light from it shone down on him like a beacon.

Buster wrestled the can along, pushing it toward the tall writing. Now the theme park's former parking lot was visible, cracking in spots with grass growing through the gaps. It was where he had parked the other night to eat his supper. He hadn't gone far, when a man came out of the shadows with a bag tossed over his back. It was the bum he had given the Cluster Cluck to, minus the biscuit.

The man eyed him for a moment. "Man, you're the chicken guy from before."

"Yep," Buster said.

"You look like you need some chicken now. You know, that chicken would have been better with a biscuit."

"Don't bet on it."

"What you doin' out here pushing a garbage can around. You some kind of clean-up crew?"

"At this time of morning? What do you think?"

"You a little testy."

"I'm a man without a place to stay, no money, and I might be a giant lizard."

"Shit, man, whatever you're on, you got to get off of it. Here."

The man swung his bag off his shoulder and dug around in it. He brought out an apple. There were a couple of bites out of it.

"Someone's done been at it, but it's clean. I got it in some kid's box lunch that was in the dumpster out back of the high school."

The man handed Buster the apple. A few hours before, he wouldn't have considered eating such a thing, but now, it made his mouth water. Buster immediately bit into it, let the juice run down his throat as he slowly and thankfully chewed the pulp.

"You thinking of going inside that ark to sleep, don't do it. That place done packed with ghosts. Ain't no one on the bum in their right mind goes in there. Besides, the gate's locked. You want in there, you got to climb the fucking wall."

"Thanks for the tip."

"Hey, I got a few places I got to check in town, for break-fast tomorrow, so I'm heading out. My name is Hadrian."

"Like the wall?"

"The what?"

"The wall the Romans built."

"Did they now?"

"It was kind of a thing."

"Say it was."

"Yep. Quite the event."

"Well, I got to go, I don't, them bums will be all over that dumpster I got in mind."

"Thanks for the apple. And my name is Buster."

"Nice meeting you, Buster. Keep it hanging loose."

Hadrian went away, his bag slung over his shoulder. Buster pushed the can over to the wall, sat down under the Brenda remarks and rested his back against the bricks and ate the rest of that apple. In that moment, he felt it was the best meal he had ever had, and that Hadrian was the best friend he ever had. Come to think of it, his life hadn't exactly been full of friends. He figured the kids who used to throw water balloons at him and call him fatty didn't count. And there was that whole thing with the dart game in sixth grade. He still had the scars.

After a momentary rest, Buster stood and looked up at the wall. Ghosts didn't scare him, and before that little moment at the séance, he hadn't believed in them, or anything that could be considered supernatural. Now he wasn't so sure. Hell, at least his life was less static. He was reasonably sure he had turned into a lizard. That was new.

He concentrated on trying to make it happen again.

Nothing. The best he could get was a soft release of gas from the strain.

Buster pushed the can along the side of the building. The wall was tall and covered in vines. The summit of the wall must have been forty feet tall.

He considered what it would take to get up it.

And then he felt it. A strange sensation of filling up with gas, but it was heavy gas, the way he had felt when he had awakened before, and now there was a ripping sound, then a shadow in the moonlight, at the edge of his vision, a large tail swishing vigorously, like a dog being offered a bone. The tail had ripped through the seat of his pants.

He took off his shirt quickly, and no sooner had he tossed it into the garbage can, than his chest swelled and his hands tingled. Then his hands were huge and his fingers were long, tipped with curved claws. He looked down at his feet. He hadn't even felt it, but his feet had swollen out of his shoes and his toes were long and his nails scraped the ground. What was left of his shoes were rips of leather.

A surge of strength, like the swell of the ocean at high tide, rose within him. He made a noise in his throat that was somewhere between a growl and a howl, and ran toward the wall, dragging the trash can behind him.

He sprang, reached out with one clawed hand, and grabbed at the bricks with a scraping noise, and then his back feet clawed their way up. With his free hand, he pulled the trash can after him. It was as light as an empty Cluster Cluck box.

He scurried up the wall like… Well, like a lizard.

When he reached the top of it, he sprang effortlessly over the side, tugging the trash can after him. There was a wide shelf of a walk up there with the wall on one side and an ornate railing on the other. The walk was eight feet wide. He pulled his trash can over to the railing and looked down. He was on what would be considered the top deck of a three-deck craft, at least in a theme park sense. Buster went along the walk quietly. He had learned he could not only move swiftly now, but near silently, though the trash can he was dragging behind him was less quiet.

He went down a staircase of brick, a railing on either side. Signs on both sides of the rail said, "Watch your step. God looks after you, but we don't."

When he reached the bottom of the steps, he went down another flight of steps toward the second deck. There was a wide, wooden double door there, and in front of it was a man with a long white beard dressed in a robe with a permanent smile on its face. He had a crooked cane in one hand.

Buster approached the bearded figure. When he was within six feet of it, it raised its right hand, the one without the staff, and gently waved, said, "TWO BY TWO. WATCH YOUR STEP."

Buster moved closer. Noah swiveled on his stand, said, "PEOPLE DID NOT COME FROM MONKEYS."

Buster walked even closer to the device. He realized then, it was his movement that activated it, caused it to spin on its stanchion, and speak with rubbery lips that coiled and pursed like fat, red worms on a hot rock.

"ENJOY THE PARK. RIDE A DINOSAUR LIKE YOUR ANCESTORS. DINOSAURS ARE ONLY FOUR THOUSAND YEARS OLD. DON'T FORGET TO CHECK OUT THE GIFT SHOP AND EMPORIUM."

Buster looked out over the park. There were water rides that were no longer activated, as well as frozen automaton dinosaurs of indeterminate breeds. One, perhaps a Brontosaurus, had a smiling cave man on its back wearing a leopard skin loin cloth.

There were other rides as well. One said "THE DROP TO HELL." It was a tall tower with an elevator, and at the top of the tower was a ride composed of half-a-dozen bucket seats and lock-in bars.

Another sign said "GARDEN OF EDEN." Buster could see what looked like plastic trees erected inside of that section. One of the trees had big, red, plastic apples hanging on it, and coiled around the tree was a fat snake, obviously made of rubber.

Looking to the bow of the ark, for that was how the park was shaped, Buster could see two large wooden doors of the sort you might find at the front of a castle.

Buster wheeled and headed along the second-floor runway toward a door not far behind Noah. It appeared to be the entrance to one of the deck houses. It had a sign over it. "VISIT THE ANIMALS, TWO BY TWO."

And then he felt funny, almost sick to his stomach. He felt like a zeppelin losing helium. He wasn't sure how it was happening, but slowly he was transforming again. With each step, he became more human and less lizard. A brisk wind cooled his ass through the rip in his pants, breezed his bare chest.

As he moved on, Noah turned slightly, said, "GET READY FOR THE FLOOD. IT'LL BE A GULLY WASHER."

INSIDE, the moonlight was shining through a grimy sun/moon roof, and there were animal hutches along the walls. Buster pushed the trash can aside. The moonlight hit Buster and made a shadow on the wall, and Buster noticed something mystifying. His shadow against the wall didn't match. It was of his lizard form, and he had already changed back to his human shape. It was another mystery, and one he was forced to compartmentalize to maintain sanity. But even as he put it in a compartment, the shadow reformed to shape into his current condition—human.

There was a wide gap in the wall just beyond a row of animal hutches. Off to the left, discernible through wide-open, double doors, partially visible in the moonlight, wearing rags of shadows, there was a pile of roller skates and a small roller rink with an ocean-blue floor. In the moonlight he could make out a sign that said, "GLIDE LIKE JESUS ACROSS THE WATER."

He could make out now that there were artificial animals and birds, two by two, in the large cages along the wall. There were signs on them just in case of confusion. They said "GOATS, PIGS, DOVES."

In the back he could barely make out the cages and the animal shapes there. The moonlight was not strong enough at the rear of the cabin. But the cages were larger, and he was reasonably certain there were a couple of shadowy horses and a pair of giraffes.

As Buster moved forward, his movement set off an electronic eye, or some such, and the goats bleated, the pigs grunted, and the doves in the cages flapped their wings. There were some weaker noises from the rear, as if the batteries in those critters had almost worn down, but the doves rose from the floor of their cages and flapped their way to the top of their coops like real doves, then settled down.

Something in the dark animal quarters to the rear of the cabin moved. Buster saw a shape, and then the shape froze. Buster squinted into the darkness. The shape had not moved in an electronic fashion, but in the more fluid motions of a human being.

"Who's there? Come out and show yourself."

Slowly, a boy about fourteen stepped out of the shadows. He had dark skin and wild hair. He looked to have been dressed by a friendly scarecrow. All he was missing was straw sticking out of his sleeves and pants legs.

"I was expecting you," the boy said. "Expecting me? Who the hell are you?"

"Isaac. Socrates said you were coming."

"Socrates? The philosopher?"

"The chicken."

Buster waited for a punchline that wasn't coming.

"Said you called him Socks."

"Socks the chicken told you I was coming?"

"That's right."

That's when something low down to the floor moved out of the darkness and into the slash of moonlight.

It was Socks. He looked a little rough. His feathers were singed and he had a black patch over one eye.

"You look like shit," said the chicken.

"Shit," Buster said. "I thought the chicken spoke. You a ventriloquist there, boy?"

"I put words in my own beak," said the chicken. "Tell him, kid."

Isaac shrugged. "He puts words in his own beak."

Buster's mouth fell open.

"But how can you talk? Why are you here? And how do you two know one another? How did you know I was coming?"

"Only question missing there is what is the meaning of life. But me and Isaac, we go way back. Went to school together and graduated Magna Cum Laude. I wrote all his papers though."

"I was home-schooled," Isaac said, "and I met this chicken today."

"It was a joke," Socks said. "Shit, you know a joke when you hear it, don't you?"

"And there's something else," Isaac said, as he turned to leave the room.

"I thought you were blown up," Buster said to Socks.

"I thought *you* were. Glad we both made it, though I got a limp that seems to come and go, blind in one eye, got weak bowels. Still, I'm better in most ways. Watch this."

The chicken sat on his ass and used a foot to adjust his eye patch. "I can also peel a banana. I got some dexterity out of the deal. Oh, and I'm connected with demons. I told them Socks was short for Socrates, like I'm him in chicken form. They seem to have bought it. I didn't want them to think I was just about laying eggs and pecking shit."

Buster thought: *Okay, I'm still in the hospital and I'm drugged and I'm not actually in a Noah's Ark theme park talking to some kid and a chicken.*

Buster pinched his own cheek. It hurt.

"But how are you so smart?" Buster said. "That's insulting."

"Sorry. I don't mean to-"

"I'm just busting your balls. It was a shitty security spell gone wrong kind of thing. Guys sacrifice chickens, say a few spells, make a few promises, demons are set loose to kill five victims, and then the people who do the spell, they get a successful five years, then they got to sacrifice again at the end of those five years, or the demons start looking for them. You don't want that. That can really suck. Elroy, he's the head of that little séance group. The Spell Boys, I call them, as of just now, by the way. You fucked things up for them, Buster. You deep-fried those demon worshiping asshats and the spell got big-time goobered up. Now the survivor, because there is one, Elroy, ole chicken king himself, he has to finish what the demon was going to do or he goes to a not very nice place and has to boil in hot doo-doo or some such thing until the sun burns out. Maybe longer than that. That's not like a long weekend, man. That's some serious time."

"I bet. Things have been pretty strange on this side as well. Seems I might also have gotten that creepy lizard guy inside me."

"Well, it might be the least of your worries. You got the attributes of that lizard dude, well, some of them, not all the magic spell-casting stuff he can do, but you got some lizard abilities, buddy. You're going to fucking need them. Elroy said he's coming. He was in demon land with me for a while. We didn't exactly hang, but I saw him, I heard him. Now that I think about it, I think we smoked cigars together. I mean, hell, you don't get a lot of choices who you hang with in that place. Chickens kind of got to stick together. Bleak, baby, that's what I'm trying to tell you."

"Wait. Elroy? The chicken guy is an actual chicken?"

"Oh, you're awake now. Good. You see, when things went explody and lizardy for you, our pal Elroy grew some feathers, and became the biggest, ugliest chicken I ever did see. And he had to spend time at Hell's gate."

"Elroy's a chicken?"

"Wow. Time travel. Or was that just the same fucking question twice? Elroy's a rooster. Kind of had to keep my eye on him. He kept talking about busting some eggs."

"But you sound like... a male."

"Transgender shit, Bubby. Maybe you've heard of it. Male born in a female's body, that's me."

"You remember me talking to you in the chicken yard?"

"I was different, but when the explosion gave me some

smarts, some of what you told me came back to me. It wasn't exactly stimulating stuff, want to know the truth, but I remember a lot of it. Did you actually masturbate to a Farrah Fawcett poster you had?"

"I never said that."

"Did too. But listen, who you pulled your meat to isn't the problem here. Me being a smart fucking chicken worked out, though I lost an eye in the deal. That's on you, you clumsy fucker."

"They were going to cut your throat, Socks."

"Got me there. Yeah, thanks. You did me a solid. Elroy, he's been sacrificing for years. Family tradition. Why else do you think a fucked-up idea like Pick-A-Chicken would catch on. Magic, baby. Black magic. He gives the demon lizard a sacrifice of chickens, spells and such, and the demon lizard kills enough humans to complete a kind of internal spell. I don't know, demon office politics or some shit. Anyway, that satisfies the lizard fucker. Who'd think that was a thing? Then he goes back to the demon house and grants some wishes, prosperity to those who get him across the line for a while. He gets some kills, sucks some souls, and Elroy's family line keeps on making money off inferior chicken recipes."

"Why didn't I go to Hell's Gate?"

"Spell wasn't yours. It was Elroy's. The Lizard Demon had to read him the riot act for fucking things up, gave him a time limit to set things straight. He don't, well the Lizard Lord loses some of his juice until someone else gets that spell book and casts a similar spell to profit. And who knows, there may never be another. That spell book has been in Elroy's family for centuries. All the way back to the old country, when they were living in the hills fucking sheep. Something about the Lizard Lord coming into our world gives him some kind of extra power, more juice in the badlands when he goes home. I don't know. Kind of vague, really, which is not too unlike a lot of that stupid spell stuff."

"I didn't go to the Hell Gate, but you did. Why?"

"Close proximity is my guess. Who knows?"

Isaac returned, holding the tome from the night of the explosion. A light green mist lazily drifted from between the pages and floated in the air and dissolved.

"Does that every time you open it," Isaac said. "The chicken found it, had me get it for him."

"Yeah" Buster said. "I remember that book. Elroy was quoting a spell from it."

"You know, that's the book I was talking about, right?" Socks said.

"Oh," Buster said.

"Despite my increase in intellect, I still can't carry a giant book. No thumbs. But I spotted Isaac here digging through the wreckage and he was kind enough to do the heavy lifting."

"I was pretty surprised," Isaac said. "You know, a talking chicken and all. I was just looking for something I could use here. Scrounging. How I survive. And he told me there was this guy we would be seeing. He was talking about you. I realized when you came in, I'd seen you before, sitting out in the parking lot in a wreck of a car."

"The night I gave Hadrian the chicken meal."

"Yeah. That was nice of you." Isaac said. "But, like I was saying, a talking chicken. And Socks saying you would show up, and well, here you are. He also said you might be a lizard."

"I had a premonition," Socks said. "I got a few powers like that from my time in demon world. That spell gave me some smarts and a few abilities that aren't common, especially for a chicken."

"I bet," Buster said.

"Spell that held me down there, it had a clock on it, parts

of it anyway. The part where I'm in demon land. That went away. I got to thank you for that too. You fucked their spell up, and I'm part of the fuck up. Hell's Gate, some kind of dimensional thing, I figure, not actual magic. Science-magic, but let's not hurt your head here. Thing is, there were two places you could go. Back here, or through Hell's Gate into permanent discomfort. Like having to listen to elevator music all the time, only hotter. Some do all right down there, get good jobs. Royal ass-wiper, that kind of thing. I was the right height, so it was something I was considering. But then I got jerked back up here. Air's better, opportunities a little less dismal. Got to say, though, all that heat, I think it was better for my skin. Pores are definitely more open. Can feel it under my feathers. Thing is, you and me, since we've been touched by the spell, we got to make sure the big chicken doesn't succeed in doing what the Lizard Demon was supposed to do. He's kind of got that assignment himself, the kills, you see, Elroy makes chicken sacrifices normally, Lizard Demon, he does the five whacks. Things have changed due to the fucked- up spell. Lizard Demon now has to depend on a fried chicken salesman. Lizard Demon can't come back up here any time soon, not the way that spell got twisted. If Elroy doesn't succeed with the killings it's going to be a hot time for him for eternity, which is only a little longer than a poetry reading. Virgil is down there. Painful shit. Never shuts up. Aeneas did this, Aeneas did that.

"Another thing: we got to stop Elroy, or we don't get to stay up here. We're connected to the spell. Elroy wins, we not only lose here, our souls travel to the hot place. We do win, we're free to continue as we are. Me a talking chicken trapped in a female body when I feel like a male. By the way, please use the pronoun 'he.'"

Buster felt dizzy and confused. He unconsciously stepped back, and the mechanical doves in the cages rose again. They fluttered, then settled down while cooing. Now that his eyes had adjusted, Buster could see the doves were attached to rods they could slide up and down on. "You know," Socks said. "I got quite a few skills out of all this. Nice sense of direction. The visions. I can do some complicated math shit. I also got this feeling, like maybe I wanted to, I could tap dance."

Socks didn't break into a dance to affirm this.

Buster said, "I think maybe I need to sit down for a while."

Buster sat on the floor, the cold tile cooling his ass where it poked through his ripped clothes.

"What about the book?" Buster asked.

Isaac opened it again, left it open. The green mist rose again, only thicker this time, like green cotton candy. Then the mist gathered into a green spear of wavering light and shot directly into Socks' bad eye, going right through the eye patch.

Socks flapped his wings rapidly, let out a squawk and a stream of shit shot out of his ass. He staggered to the left, then to the right, as if he had finally decided to test his dancing abilities.

"Goddamn it to hell," Socks said.

Socks turned to face the wall, lifted his eye patch with a hind leg while stiffly standing on the other. From his eye came a beam of green light. It danced and flickered on a barren spot of the wall. In the glow, there were shadowy images, and slowly the images took shape in black and white.

It revealed one big chicken, a rooster, as big as Buster was when he was a lizard.

The light on the wall that held the images sputtered, and wavered. The Big Rooster was coming up from the bank of the creek, a spot near where Buster had been this very night. Color bled into the black and white scene and there was a silver glow from the moon and they could see the big chicken was orange and black with a fluttering red comb on his head. Near him was a candy-apple red convertible parked next to the creek bank. Its top was down. There was a man and a woman in the convertible, kissing.

It was a lover's lane.

The two in the car didn't notice the giant chicken. They continued to pursue a game of dueling tongues as the chicken came near.

The rooster flexed a wing, which worked as well as a hand, and reached into the convertible, clenched strangely prehensile feathers around the man's arm and pulled him out from behind the wheel. The man's pants, already around his knees, caught on the mirror and were ripped completely off. The big chicken dragged him toward the creek and down the bank, out of sight. The woman sat, stunned, her mouth wide open.

"What the hell?" Buster said.

The light in Socks' eye died. He fell over on his side, and spewed more white chicken shit.

"Jesus," Socks said, staggering to his feet. "That was one of those visions I was telling you about. Damn. I think I strained my liver or something."

"We have to help that man."

"Too late," Socks said, "but the place is near here. Like I told you, I'm good with direction. Got a kind of built in GPS."

Buster felt agitated, nervous, excited, frightened. He couldn't put a finger on the sensation, but whatever it was he felt, he was swelling, and he knew he was transforming into a lizard.

Buster trembled. He felt strong. He swished his tail.

"That's the stuff, right there," Socks said. "Though, you got to know, your water hose is on the loose."

"Let's go," Buster said, already heading toward the door. "And Socks, the mess you made, that's going to be a regular thing, we might ought to keep on hand some wet naps, or some such."

Buster was happy to see they were going downhill again. Downhill was easiest. He shuffled one foot, and then the other. He was wearing the largest pair of skates he could find from the skating rink in the ark. His heels hung off the back of the skates, but his balance as a lizard was remarkably better than when he was human.

Isaac had given him a dark blue hoodie, the hood pulled tight around his face. The hoodie had a logo across the back of it that read, "Two By Two!" He had tied a large scarf from his trash can in such a way it made a loin cloth.

As he picked up speed, the hood blew back and the wind whipped against his dry scaly head. He felt now that he knew how to transform. All he had to do was get a little worked up. It wasn't about trying hard, it was about trying a little and feeling confident.

He felt his muscles ripple under his skin like cables. He swung his tail from left to right as he went, to keep him balanced, like a ship's rudder, to stay in control of the skates as they rolled along the paved road with a sound like mice squeaking. Definitely some WD-40 was needed.

Buster saw headlights from an approaching car, peeking over the top of the next hill.

He reached back, pulled the hood over his head, adjusted it around his face.

As the car passed, he slowed, kept his head down, hoping not to be noticed.

It passed by, not giving any indication he had been spotted.

Buster looked back to see Isaac, also shuffling along on skates, still a way's back. Socks was sitting on top of Isaac's head like a hat, not too unlike the ones from the Pick-A-Chicken. Socks was pointing with her wing. Or was it his wing? He had asked to be called him instead of her. It was all kind of confusing. Chicken was good. Just call him chicken, Buster thought. Buster could see that Socks was shouting something, but Buster was too far ahead to hear it. Socks was supposed to be in the lead, but once they reached a certain spot, Buster knew where the place was, having passed it earlier that night.

That's when Buster saw the woman running down the road toward them, screaming. The woman from the convertible. She was pale of skin and blonde and really had some lungs. You could have heard her screams over a jet engine.

The woman came closer, then suddenly veered off the street, as if she had blown a tire. She collapsed partly in the road, partly on the side of it, overcome by fear and exhaustion. Buster skated over to her.

"Ma'am," Buster said. "Are you okay?"

"Big chicken," she said. "Big fucking chicken. Blood and feathers!"

Buster squatted on the ground next to the lady. The woman took a deep breath and stared hard at Buster. The moonlight was heavy on his face.

She screamed and crab-walked backwards away from him.

"What are you?" she said.

"It's okay."

"No it isn't," the woman said. "Stay back!"

She vibrated a little and eased down until she lay stiff on the ground, having passed out. Buster didn't blame her. A giant chicken and a giant lizard in one night were hard to assimilate.

"Pull her out of the road," Buster said to Isaac. "I'm going after Elroy."

THE PARTIAL MOON was full and bright and it rose above the tree line that bordered the creek like a silver scimitar. A red convertible seemed to bloom in front of Buster, and it wasn't swerving. It was bearing down on him, a big chicken at the wheel.

Buster skated around it, but had the convertible had another coat of paint, it would have hit him. The big chicken, Elroy, gave Buster a glance as he went by, stuck his middle feather up and honked the car horn.

Buster skidded on his skates, turned and glanced back. Isaac and Socks barely avoided the car as well, and were now racing to meet him.

Buster skated over the hill and to the creek, turned his attention back to where he had seen the man being carried in Socks' vision. Steam rose out of the creek. Buster took a breath, skated over to the edge, looked through the trees, clamored down the bank on the skates, almost falling over. The man was there. Or rather his corpse. The body was ripped open and the steam rising was from his intestines, hissing in the night air. His arms and legs were pulled loose of his torso as if he were a soft gingerbread man. They had been tossed into the creek.

Buster moved closer, looked at the face. The man's eyes were gone, plucked out.

Socks and Isaac slid down the creek bank to stand by Buster. Isaac had removed his skates. Now he looked at the man on the ground, bent over and threw up. "Jesus," he said.

"It's the beginning of the spell," Socks said. "Don't know exactly what's going on, but we need to get back and look at that book. I have a facility for a lot of languages now, even Sanskrit."

"That was some moment you had," Buster said.

"During that episode, I gathered a bit of this, a bit of that. Experience and knowledge runs loose in that dimension, like a flow of invisible water. A lot of it washed over me. Big

Chicken has to complete five murders in place of what Lizard Demon would have done. I know. It's weird, but hey, I don't make the rules. I think that's right, anyway. That might be something I picked up from a game show. I get a bump here and there from HBO from time to time."

"Yesterday I was just worried about the cops finding out where I was living," Isaac said. "But now I'm what, a crusader of some sort? That's kind of high profile."

"The lady in the road," Buster said. "We should see she gets to a doctor."

"She's fine," Socks said.

"She got up and ran off," Isaac said. "Yeah, she had some stride, that one did."

They heard sirens coming their way.

"Lady must have called the cops," Socks said.

"Then we better get moving," Buster said.

"Isaac strap back on those skates."

BUSTER, back in human form, leaned on the counter of the local Gas-N-Go as the clerk rang up a few items. Nothing extravagant, being all Buster had were a few wadded up bills he'd found in his trash can of belongings. But if they were going to pull an all-nighter, checking out that big book of hoodoo spells, they would need a bit of something to snack on.

Couple cheap cups of noodles for him and the kid, a loaf of bread for the chicken, some instant coffee, and some wet wipes for the aftermath of the vision, and any visions forthcoming.

The clerk, an older man with thinning hair and a gut that he propped against the counter, dragged the items across a beeping scanner as a TV blared overhead. The flickers caught the attention of Buster as he watched an attractive reporter point her microphone at first one cop, then another. Neither had anything to tell her.

Buster recognized where the reporter was. It was a news feed from a few days back. It had been playing endlessly. Not since Grover Cleveland stopped by on his way to a South Texas resort had there been this much excitement in Tiktaalik, Texas.

"And do you believe what happened to the man was part of a ritualistic killing?" she said, again pointing her microphone towards an officer who turned away from her.

But the reporter was no quitter.

"Is it true that both of his eyes were removed?"

"We need to keep this area clear," the officer said, motioning her away.

"And what about the witness accounts of a giant chicken?" she said. "Or a big lizard?"

"Yeah, right," the officer said, turned away and ducked under crime scene tape.

The clerk laughed, and Buster turned to look at him.

"Hoo boy," the clerk said. "Giant chickens and big lizards. That witness must have been smoking some of the good stuff. They keep running this shit over and over. Guess it beats politics."

Buster forced a weak chuckle and curled his lip into a half-hearted grin.

BUSTER WALKED into the Ark with his plastic bag sporting the Gas-N-Go logo. He made his way into what was once an employee break room.

Socks hopped up on the table as he walked in. "Hope you had a fruitful hunt," Socks said.

Buster pulled the bread out of the bag, said, "This is for you."

"Bread?" Socks said. "I look like a duck?"

"You don't like bread?" Buster said.

"I'm gonna eat it," Socks said. "I just wanted some meat, maybe a little tomato and lettuce. Would it have killed you to have got a few slices of bologna? Maybe a jar of peanut butter. You don't even have teeth to eat bologna."

"Point taken."

"Hey, is it bad that I really want to try fried chicken? You know, like from Pick-A-Chicken? That's a little fucked up, right?"

Isaac entered the room. He was wiping his hands with a rag. His face was smeared with grease.

"What in the world have you been doing?" Buster said.

"How do you think I keep this place running. I was greasing some gears, literally. I also got a riding mower down there I work on from time to time. Might be a way to turn it into transportation."

"You did all this?" Buster said. "Kept it running yourself?"

"Doesn't happen by magic," Socks said. "The kid's smart, an electrician, a grease monkey, a plumber, you name it, kid can do it. Found that out when we first met up."

"I been meaning to ask," Buster said. "You knew I was coming because of the vision, but what about Isaac? How did you know he'd help you?"

"I didn't know anything. Hell, I was staggering around out there in the Pick-A-Chicken parking lot with smoking feathers and a missing eye. He got me patched up, literally. This eye patch isn't a fashion statement. Then I had the visions about how you would come here. I had come back from Hell's Gate because you fucked up that spell, and how. They couldn't hold me. My chicken body had been blown in the fucking trees, and in what seemed longer at the Gate, was only a short time here. I started wandering around the lot, figuring out I wasn't just a hen anymore, knowing too I was a guy trapped in a broad's body, so to speak."

"When he first spoke to me," Isaac said, "I was frightened."

"Yeah, but he got over it quick."

"So why are you here, Isaac?" Buster said.

"There was a preacher, leader of what I now know is a cult. I was born into it. Preacher's name was Lawrence Murgatroyd, but he told us to call him Prophet Larry. He had inherited money, and one night he said he was drunk and fell off his porch and hit his head, and had a vision from God. God told him to honor him by building an ark, and to open it to the public, and to build an inner sanctum and to gather followers who could prepare for the rapture. It was a mix of Old Testament, New Testament, and Reverend Larry's vision. He had this ark park built. He and his followers planned to wait here for the rapture while the ark honored God and brought in money.

"Thing was, it didn't bring in that much money. My father, Abraham, was a true believer, among the Super Deacons, as they were called. He was a jack of all trades, a former engineer who had come to work here to prepare the ark for tourists, and to learn the truth of the universe from Prophet Larry. My dad and this place is all I knew. My mom had died in childbirth. My friends were the children of followers. There weren't that many, by the way. We could hardly get enough gathered for a baseball team."

"Here comes the good part," Socks said.

"Prophet Larry, he's up on a ladder one day, changing light bulbs. Happened right over there. He got to wobbling on the ladder, fell off and hit his head and went into a coma for three days. The cult, which to me was just a religion then, didn't believe in doctors. Then, one day, he rose up suddenly, said, 'Damn. That was some fall.'

"His followers were gathered around his bed, and they said it was a miracle. But, Larry, he said, 'No such thing. I just got better. And you know all that stuff I told you about, that knock on the head straightened me out. It was bullshit.

There ain't no rapture, and I built this ark for nothing. We can't even fill it up come summer if we offered free admission and a hand job.'

"Prophet Larry asked from then on that we just call him Larry. He made out a will where my father, who was his closest follower, would inherit the ark and the property and any bills that went with it, picked up his hat, kicked over one of the animal exhibits on the way out the door. He started an edible panty line that's done well for him, and I hear he's all right in the stock market."

"Heard that too," Buster said. "I know who he is from the television and the papers. Those panties come in all colors and one rainbow blend."

"My dad was devastated. He thought Larry had lost his way, and his bullshit was still true. For my dad, it had to be. The followers drifted off. My dad as a leader couldn't hold a statue's attention. The cult died out. Dad decided the rapture was waiting on him. Out there, on the deck, he climbed up on the rampart, spread his arms, and flew away. For a moment. Then he went straight to the ground and it killed him. Long story short, the will had a clause in it that if something happened to my dad, I owned the property. Some things were repossessed. They closed the park. But I stayed. I learned about the maintenance from my dad, so I just kept enough of the place going to live here. Electricity. Plumbing. But I'm off the grid. Stealing electricity and water, because I know how. I try not to use more than I need. I scrounge about for things I want, pawn some of the stuff that was left here when the cult broke down. I don't turn on lights near the portholes unless I have them covered, stay to myself, tinkering downstairs in my dad's old shop, mostly on that old riding lawn mower. Dad used to cut a little patch of grass between the Garden of Eden and the dinosaur ride with it. Some kind of sentimental connection, I suppose. That's it. The whole story."

"And a sad one it is," Socks said. "I think, right effort had been made, the park would have worked, and you could have fleeced those dumb religious fucks for all they had. I think maybe you and me should look into that, kid."

"No thanks," Isaac said. "I may not believe Larry anymore, but I believe I should be a positive force in the universe."

"Telling you, kid. You're missing out on a gold mine. Being rich, that's pretty positive."

"No thanks, Socks," Isaac said. "I'm fine the way I am."

FROM THE DAILY TIKTAALIK

DEATH AT LOVER'S LANE
Opinion piece by: Woody Burns

New murder committed in the same bloody manner as the past. The previous victims have been homeless, or those on the edge of social acceptance. This time the murder was of an upscale individual, owner of several car lots, James Ferguson. He and his girlfriend Evelyn Potter, parked at a known lover's lane overlooking a local creek, and were attacked by what the survivor, Ms. Potter, swears had to be a man in a chicken suit.

The body of Mr. Ferguson was found on the creek bank, mutilated with his eyes missing. Ms. Potter said she abandoned the red Chevrolet convertible and made an attempt to run for help.

She claims to have been accosted by a man in a lizard suit who was in the accompaniment of an African-American male who she estimated to be in his teens, along with a chicken wearing an eye patch.

She said the lizard and his friends spoke to her, though she doesn't recall what was said. She thought the young man might be a ventriloquist, though she said she saw the little chicken's mouth move.

This strange murder, except for the social elevation of the victim, is remarkably like a series of gruesome events that have occurred for several years, and that I have reported on previously.

What is going on here? Can't the police do their job and uncover what appears, at this point, to be a cult of brutal killers, possibly involved in Satanic worship? And what's with the chicken and lizard suits? And a kid using ventriloquism to make a chicken seem to talk? Why? Who? And for that matter, what, the cluck is going on?

EARLIER: ELROY CUZZINS/BIG CHICKEN

The wind whipped through Elroy's feathers as he pulled onto the main drag in his convertible. Well, his convertible as of moments ago.

He was happy to rid the world of that guy. He had seen him in the Pick-A-Chicken drive-through many times over the years, flashing his fancy car and beautiful woman about, and frankly, his happiness had disgusted Elroy. Now the car was his. And his eyes. His woman didn't seem interested, but there was still time for her to change her mind.

The newly acquired eyes taken from the previous owner were resting in a nearby Pick-A-Chicken box that Elroy had brought with him. He assumed the stray salt granules in the bottom of it wouldn't affect the spell once all the ingredients were gathered. From past experience, you got the right stuff together, said the spell, you could mix shit and a presidential pardon with it and the result would be the same. Five more years of success for the spell caster or casters.

But the goods needed to be just that, good. Eyes are resilient, but they don't do well bouncing around in someone's pocket. Not that Elroy even had pockets.

He was covered from head to toe in feathers making

pants uncomfortable at best. That's why he didn't wear any. Not when he was a chicken.

As he started to pick up speed, he noticed a figure in the road ahead. Damn. It was a lizard. On skates. A big fucking lizard. Jesus Christ. Then things fell into place. Had to be the fat-ass security guard. He'd gotten some of the Lizard Demon's mojo. Suckarama. Knew that guy was trouble. Shouldn't have hired his porky ass.

And then there was a kid skating behind him with a fucking chicken on his shoulder. Looked like it would be a good one for the deep fryer, maybe one for a Cluck It Up box. Was that chicken wearing an eye patch? The little chicken. Shit, he remembered him from the Hot Place, talking shit, called himself Socrates, and then his spell time ended and he came back. Hated that little blow hard. The kid? Who the fuck knows?

Elroy pressed his talon a little harder on the accelerator. A grin tried its best to curl the corners of his beak, but was unsuccessful; still, he felt it inside.

Just as he was about to hit the lizard, he yelled, "Cocksucker," but the word was stolen by the wind, and at the last moment the damn lizard wheeled aside on the skates.

Elroy stuck his middle feather up at them as the convertible darted by. Deal with him later. He had fresh eyes to deal with.

Elroy parked his car between large piles of rubble. Rubble that once made up the flagship Pick-A-Chicken location. The fence that had surrounded the place had been knocked flat, and the blast had destroyed most of the supporting structures. The few pieces that had withstood the blast would have to be torn down and rebuilt. He got this spell business straightened out, was cruising again, he'd rebuild, bigger and better, maybe change it so you could pot-shot the chickens with small caliber weapons.

Now that was an idea. Shoot the head off with the chicken on the run, you got an extra biscuit, maybe. He was always coming up with fresh ideas.

As to the damage, there was an exception. The guard shack. He had been living there, brought a few items from his home where he no longer wanted to stay. Too big. Too sad. The shack had survived in total, except for a gap in the wall where the blast had driven a chicken through it. Possibly what's left of it in the next county over.

Elroy swung himself over the door of the convertible without bothering to open it, leaned back in and grabbed the chicken box, tucked it under his arm.

Inside the shack, Elroy set the box with the eyes on a nearby shelf, then reached down and picked up a pair of overalls that he brought from home, wore to relax.

Elroy focused on a spot on the wall, tilted his head, and began to molt, his feathers dropping around him, his strength and other attributes falling away, leaving him standing there in human form, potbellied and limp-dicked.

He slipped into the overalls and stretched his body. The overalls were way too large, but they were comfortable. But being in the small shack, after being in chicken form, made him feel cooped up. He thought there was a joke in there somewhere.

He sat down at the little writing desk and pulled out a small journal and a pencil, more items he had brought from home. Both pencil and journal had pictures of little cartoon chickens on them, straight from the gift shop of the Pick-A-Chicken. Or the former gift shop. It was now scattered all over Tiktaalik, Texas. Maybe somebody had a pencil up their ass, or had lost an eye. It pleased Elroy to think so.

Elroy opened the journal, turned the pages. There were multiple journal entries from his pre-chicken empire days, but he no longer enjoyed reading about how he had got a laugh out of the lady cashier. How he longed for recognition and a parade in his honor. He had managed those things through his chicken empire, but found he felt just the same as he had always felt at the core. Empty and unsatisfied. He was no longer interested in human interaction at all. Now he had the spell to worry about, had a list to make.

He put the pencil to his mouth and licked the tip, turned to a blank page and started making a list.

EYES
NOSE
EARS
TONGUE
FINGERS

He looked at the list, added

AND THUMBS

to the "fingers" note, then nodded and put a little check mark next to "eyes."

Done.

Elroy sat there a long time and looked at a blank page. His mind went here and there, back and forth. And then he began to write.

ELROY'S JOURNAL

SOMETIMES LATE AT NIGHT, WHEN THE WIND HOWLS AROUND THE HOUSE, I THINK MAYBE I FUCKED UP WHEN I MADE THE WHOLE DEMONIC DEAL.

It's changed things for me. Before I had the money, I had it simple, a girlfriend named Charlotte. Sweet. I loved her. She loved me. But my daddy always told me, "A man without money is like a man without a nut sack. He ain't a man. And if you got money, well, you get to use the dick more often. Money, he said, attracts women like dog hair to a wool suit."

But Charlotte. She was a sweetie. She was a second skin, fit me just right. I thought of something, said something, she was already in line with me, could finish my sentences, and add a better ending.

Then my old man, when I turned thirty, he came to me, all bones and skin like leather, his bald head shiny as a boiled egg, and said, "Elroy, I haven't got long left. I have a piper to pay, but I thought I'd pass on a legacy to you, and I don't just mean fried chickens and biscuits, not to mention coleslaw. How would you like to be so lucky that if you fell in a vat of lava it would only moisten your skin? How would you like some tall-ass blonde in high heels with a butt cocked up like it had a floor jack under it, come walking by, and she sees you, and bam, you look to her like a fucking movie star? You could have her any way you wanted her, and tomorrow, after she's waxed your dick, you could discard her and find another big-tittied, long-legged home-wrecker who could squat and pick up a dime with her asshole and give you change, and a coupon for Tuesdays."

"But there's Charlotte," I said to the old man.

"That bony, bug-eyed bitch with the knock knees, always in flat heels with her hair pinned back? Hell no, boy. That's donkey love. And what the fuck does love have to do with it, comes right down to it? Love don't buy you a Cadillac car, a house with a pool and sauna. A maid and a butler, and hair implants that look as natural as a fucking sunset. Do what I tell you, you'll thrive, be farting through silk undies. That's how it's been for me these last thirty years. Think I miss your mother? She's working packing tuna fish in Maine, and all she got out of me in the divorce was my best wishes and some kind of rash. You think I miss that one fucking chicken shack on a back street? Think I miss all that lame-ass shit when I got a goddamn empire now? And with a few easy spells, you could take my place. It's about spells and soul-selling, and way I see it the soul ain't nothing but an idea and a shadow. But money, that stuff spends, and everything you might want of flesh or stone, bone or steel, it comes to you with money. You'll step on a few toes. You'll have a few enemies. But think of it this way. You're the one fucking everyone else over, not the one being fucked over. Are you in?"

It was a lot, and I thought it over. One day I woke up and there was Charlotte lying beside me, her mouse-colored hair tied back and held in place with a scrunchie, and I'm working at one of my dad's chicken places, cooking chicken in a wire basket, dipping it in hot grease that's popping on my wrist, watching through a window as folks hatchet the shit out of chickens in the yard, and I'm thinking, so this is the job Dad gave me, and now he's telling me I can be a rich, swinging-dick who has some other schmuck cooking the chicken while I pile in the long green doodah, I thought, you know, that might not be a bad way to go.

I hated leaving Charlotte though. Only way I could get rid of her was tell her I didn't love her. And I did. It hurt at first, but Dad said I'd get over it, and so would she. I was going to be a little god on earth.

So, Dad has me come to the meeting place, at the Red House, and I take my place around a circle with drawings in it, and then he has some of his workers there, and some chickens, and he teaches me this ritual, and I'm in. It was scary. It was disturbing, but oh, the power that spell gave me. Electricity jumped through my head and the lights dimmed and the walls got close and the ground opened, and the next thing I know I'm wearing my birthday suit standing amidst a bunch of steam, and there's the Lizard Demon, green and scaly, piss-yellow eyes, and a toothy grin. And for me, it had begun.

I felt powerful. I felt good. Week later, I'm working in the main office, making decisions that all turn out right, 'cause, you see, I got the Lizard Demon's grant now, and Dad came in, closed the door, said, "Might ought to mention this again, because you'll need to mark your calendar and keep it in mind. Things are good for you now, but every five years, you got to show up at the Red House, and you'll need to know the renewal spell. Do that, things are fine. But, one little catch, and I mentioned this, but I think maybe I ought to elaborate on it now, and it's this. I have passed on what would have happened to me to you. How it works. Got to have a foil, and I love you, Son, but like your dear old mother working in the tuna factory, it's not about her. It's not about you. It's about me. I've swapped the debt. Something you can do too when you get close to the Big Casino, but that patsy, person, must accept it willingly. If not, well, away you go where it's hot and damp. One nice thing. You do good up here, over there, down there, wherever there in the Hot Land, you might get some kind of executive job, something without the eternal pain. And maybe not. Folks in the Hot Land, they can be wishy-washy once you get there. A visit is fine, but permanent residence, well, you get a ghetto section for that. Sorry to fuck you over, but hey, that's the name of the game, boy. Hey, got to go. Dinner tonight at the Red Hedge Inn? They're serving that ham."

I trembled. I cried. I wished I'd stayed home with Charlotte.

But only for a moment.

Because of Buster Nix, fat-ass dick-head, everything is all in a tumble. I owe that goddamn Buster some hard business, that's for sure.

I found documents and a photograph in the shack after Buster was gone. There was a sticky note stuck to the job document, one for the job here. Sticky note read: "Good luck, Buster, Auntie June."

The document was signed by a June Nix. And on Buster's desk was a framed photo of him and a plump, brown woman with a sweet smile.

I figured Auntie June was the woman in the photo, the one that wrote the note. Guy like Buster, how many friends could he have? How many relatives could stand him? He was the kind of guy had to put lard on his balls to get the dog to lick them.

So yeah, that was her. That was Auntie June. Oh, Auntie June. You better watch out.

AUNT JUNE

JUNE slowly and carefully made her way up the staircase to her apartment. The stairs had never been great for her, and as the years passed, they had only gotten harder. Her bad knees didn't make it easy, and carrying her purse looped over her arm by its strap, as well as clutching a bag of groceries had added to the challenge. She felt that in the next few years, she might have to consider some place on a lower level.

The trick was to take her time with each stair.

It was slow going, moving with all the concentration of a mountain climber reaching a precarious and icy summit. Checking to make sure her footing was good enough to prevent her from tumbling backwards and sending her and the contents of her grocery bag into the air, running the risk of not only injury, but her plans for dinner as well. Maybe she could hire a Sherpa guide to lead the way with a rope attached.

Only a few steps left.

A voice from behind startled her a little, but fortunately she had the cloth grocery bag by the straps in one hand, and her other hand was clutching the guard rail. She glanced over her shoulder, saw a man wearing a long buttoned up coat; it came to his ankles, the collar button was fastened. The man stood at the bottom of the stairs, smiling at her. She had once seen a still from an old silent film titled *The Man Who Laughs*, and at that moment, the man at the bottom of the stairs looked just like that; big frozen smile in a strained, bony face.

"Damn, man. Almost shit myself."

"Didn't mean to startle you. Need some help there Mrs. Nix?"

"You're that chicken guy." June tried to recall his name. "Ellis something."

"Elroy Cuzzins," stepping up on the stairs and taking the bag for June.

"Cuzzins," she said. "That's right. Buster was working for you, but if you're here looking for that nephew of mine, no one's seen him or heard from him since the hospital. Frankly, I'm worried. I fear he might be dead in a ditch somewhere. He had some bad burns."

"He's not dead," Elroy said.

"Oh?"

"I came over to tell you he's alive, so you can stop worrying. Let me help you put these in your apartment, and I'll explain."

June dug around in her purse until she came up with a set of keys, slipped one into her door. Elroy followed her inside.

"We just need to discuss some legal matters, your nephew and I," Elroy said. "And he told me I might best talk to you about it."

"What sort of legal matters could I help with?"

"Shall we set these groceries down?"

They made their way down the hall of her tiny apartment. Modest in size, several little Hummels and tchotchkes covered shelves and counters.

June motioned to a counter near the kitchen, took a seat

in the old armchair positioned in front of a small TV. She let her purse rest in her lap.

"I gotta sit," June said. "That climb ain't doing anything good for these old knees."

Elroy placed the bag on the counter, took a peek inside. He saw a bag of cookies; chocolate coated graham crackers.

He hadn't had one of those in ages. He leaned back against the counter and silently studied June.

"Thanks for the help with the groceries," June said, "but I don't think I can help with legal matters. I know what you're doing to Buster, trying to stick him with an outrageous bill, trying to make him responsible."

"He is responsible."

"You think you're going to get eight million dollars or so out of Buster. He couldn't afford a used breath of air."

"Does he have some sort of insurance?"

"You know he doesn't. He had to answer those questions on his work application, and if you think I have eight million in my purse, you're wrong."

"Just thought there might be some kind of insurance, or that you might have some sort of savings you could contribute."

"To an eight-million-dollar bill? I don't think you thought that, Mr. Cuzzins. I think you haven't talked to Buster. I think you thought I might know where he is. You think if I did, and I don't, I'd tell you? Far as I know, he's dead."

Elroy was no longer smiling. His face was impassive. It was as if he had been turned to stone. June thought she could have struck a match on his cheek bones.

"You and him are close, aren't you?"

"I practically raised him. He's a good boy, just not the best at making life plans."

June had gently opened her purse, and now she slid her hand inside of it.

"I thank you again for helping me with the groceries, but

I'm an old lady and need to go to bed, so I'm going to have to ask you to leave."

"Yeah. Well, you can ask."

Elroy pulled the cookies out of the grocery bag, tore them open, pulled out one and took a bite.

"Damn, that's good. I used to eat these when I was a kid. I think of these cookies, I think of my mother. She left when I was young. Child of divorce. Very hard on a kid."

"Why don't you have a glass of milk," June said. "Maybe fix yourself a sandwich, shit in the toilet."

Elroy's formerly stone face was animated now. "I just might do that, but June, I got bad news for you. I'm not really here to talk about insurance, or what Buster can pay. Or what you can help him pay."

"I realize that now."

"What you got in the purse, June?"

"Come closer and I'll show you."

Elroy ate another cookie, then he stopped leaning against the counter, stood up straight.

"You remind me a bit of my mother. Wrong color skin, of course, and she wasn't short and fat like you, but you remind me of her. You have, what can I call it. I know. Motherly warmth."

"Not for you."

"No. Not for me. But you have it. At least while you're still warm. Cold, you got nothing. No warmth. No personality, and just so you know, when I finish here, I'm taking these cookies with me."

June gently pulled a small flat automatic from her purse and pointed it at Elroy.

Elroy snickered. "You get that out of a Cracker Jack box?"

"I got it at a gun store, along with the ammunition in it. Old lady, she's got to have something."

"I see."

"Looks as if your coat lining is shedding feathers there, sport."

"Oh, that," Elroy removed his coat. He was only wearing a pair of boxer shorts and his shoes, no socks. Small downy feathers fluttered in the air, floated to the floor.

"Before you leave, you'll be sweeping that up," June said. "There's a broom and dustpan in the closet. But first, put your coat back on."

June noticed the backs of Elroy's hands, wrists and lower forearms were covered in feathers, and a few were leaking from his hair. As June watched, his hand and fingers became the tip of a wing, and the feathers there parted and moved back together, parted again, as if they were fingers. The feathers were rust-colored and mixed with white.

"That some kind of magic trick?"

"Depends on how you look at it. But if you mean sleight of hand, nope. Your nephew, he's a big lizard, and I'm a large chicken, and life for neither of us will ever be the same, though I'm beginning to think this isn't so bad, except I got a piper to pay."

"You get dropped on your head?"

"Lady, I got blown all over the place, so I'm sure the head was involved, but I blame a nice visit to Hell's Gate, due to your stupid nephew."

"What kind of nonsense are you talking. Go on now, get out, and you can leave the feathers. I'll sweep them up."

By this time Elroy was covered in feathers, and his body was swelling. His face was contorting and reshaping, and where his hair had been, there was now a large, blood-red rooster comb.

Elroy reached down and pushed his boxer shorts off. If he didn't, in a moment, they'd split.

"Hey, hold your horses, creepy."

Elroy pushed a shoe off his foot using his other foot to

make it happen. Then he used that foot to push off the other shoe.

Elroy's lips pinched together and pushed forward and turned a yellow color. They grew until they were an enormous beak. Where his feet were, there were talons, big and yellow, sharp as daggers.

The weapon in June's hand sagged a bit, and then she laughed. It wasn't a laugh of humor, but one of surprise and confusion.

"I'm going to need your touch," Elroy said.

"What."

"Your fingers, dear. You might call it a metaphorical reference. Oh, the thumbs, too."

Elroy took one step forward and June fired the automatic. She might as well have thrown a pea at him. The bullet struck him and bounced off and embedded in the wall.

Elroy jumped her, knocking her and the chair backwards.

June tried to scream, but it was as if a plug was in her mouth. She was in shock. All she could do was make a kind of coughing noise.

Big Chicken pecked her throat as if his beak were a dagger.

When he lifted his head, his beak and feathers were splashed with blood.

He lifted his head and let out with a loud, "Cock-a-doodle-doo!"

And then he went to work on her fingers, tearing them and her thumbs loose with his beak.

Later, he gathered his shorts and shoes, and left with them and the bag of cookies. The walls and floor were wet and red.

"I DON'T KNOW why I have to hide in this bag," Socks said.

Socks was peering out of Isaac's backpack, which Isaac had taken off his back to adjust at the edge of an alleyway. Buster leaned against the alley wall and watched. He was holding a large cloth shopping bag with his PlayStation and games in it. "Because, I can't just carry around a talking chicken," Isaac said, "that's why."

"Well la-de-dah. Some of us can't just switch back and forth all easy and lizard-like, and are stuck in full-bore chicken gear, idling there."

"We don't make the rules," Buster said.

"Riding in a backpack is a bullshit rule."

"Actually, chickenshit. That's why you got the newborn diaper," Isaac said, zipping the backpack closed, muffling Socks' response.

"I think I like him better this way," Isaac said.

"I know I do," Buster said.

A muffled noise came from the backpack. Isaac adjusted the pack onto his back.

Buster clutched the bag with his PlayStation and games tight under his arm, and they crossed the street to Big Jake's Jewels and Pawn.

THE COWBELL on the front door clanged as Buster and Isaac, with his pack of chicken, walked inside. The air was stale with cigar smoke.

A tall fat guy, reading a magazine, was leaning on the glass counter. He wore a tent-like Hawaiian shirt decorated with colorful parrots. There was an ashtray at his elbow containing cigar stubs. Dark smoke drifted up from one of them.

"You Big Jake?" Buster said.

"I am," Jake said, glanced up, then turned his attention back down to his magazine. "You got sale or pawn goods in that pack and bag?"

"I have some things in this bag. *His* stuff is personal," Buster said.

"Can't bring that pack in here with personal items," Jake said. "I've seen that trick a few times too many, using it to stuff away goods."

"Just his schoolbooks," Buster said.

"Don't care if he's got his baby brother in there and his legs are cut off at the knees," Jake said. "Can't bring it in here. Too many people stealing my cow skulls."

Buster looked around, noted a bunch of overpriced jewelry, hedge trimmers, guns, this and that, and the top of Jake's head bent over the magazine.

"I don't see any cow skulls," Buster said.

"Exactly," Jake said. "Like I said, kid, you can leave the pack outside or have me put it behind the counter."

"I'll wait outside," Isaac said. "It'll be easier. Fresh air and all."

Buster nodded. Isaac went outside to the clatter of the cowbell over the door.

Buster approached the counter, noticing the magazine that kept Jake's attention was the latest edition of *Cat Fancy*.

"Like cats?" Buster said.

Big Jake looked at him a moment, then back at his magazine.

Buster set the bag on the counter and unpacked the PlayStation and the games. Jake didn't move.

Buster pushed the machine and the games a little closer so it touched the magazine.

Jake gave the PlayStation a sideways glance. "Thirty bucks."

"That's it?"

"I'll do forty if it comes with the games."

"A game by itself cost fifty."

A toilet in the back flushed and out walked Hadrian, wiping his hands on his pants. He saw Buster and smiled as he came around the counter.

"Well, if it ain't my chicken and no biscuit buddy," Hadrian said. "Last I saw you, you weren't looking so good."

"I don't pay you to talk, Hadrian," Jake said.

"You're right, you're right," Hadrian said.

"You did, I'd be a millionaire."

Hadrian winked at Buster, walked over and picked up a push broom propped in the corner. He started shoving it around the floor. Seemed to Buster all he was doing was redistributing the dirt. Jake said, "Look, forty-five for the PlayStation and games, and that's a final offer. I got a peppermint stick here I can give you, still in the package, but that, and my sincere hopes for a better future for us all are it."

"Aww man," Hadrian said. "I thought you said I could have that stick."

"Cash is fine," Buster said. "Go ahead and give Hadrian the peppermint."

Jake pulled a key from a retractable cord attached to his belt, unlocked a small lockbox under the desktop. He pulled out the money, placed it on the counter, locked the box back, put it away, let the keys zip back into position on his belt.

He had the peppermint stick in his shirt pocket. He plucked it out and flipped it in Hadrian's direction. Hadrian missed the catch. The peppermint scooted across the floor making a scratching noise.

"That's disrespectful," Hadrian said.

"No, that's a free peppermint," Jake said. "Shit, man, it's wrapped in plastic."

Hadrian picked it up and began to peel the plastic away. He stuck the stick in his mouth, and began to suck on it as he went back to sweeping.

Buster was folding the greenbacks and pushing them in

his pocket, when a loud grinding noise caused them all to freeze in their tracks. Then the cowbell clanged, and there in the doorway was Isaac, looking like something wet and icy had just dribbled down his back.

"There's trouble," he said.

EARLIER, ON THE STREET, WAITING ON BUSTER

Isaac unzipped the backpack and Socks stuck his head out.

"That, boy, was some disrespectful shit," Socks said.

"Sorry. Not much choice."

"Where are we, anyways?"

"Big Jake's Jewels and Pawn."

A woman walked by, carrying a baby, saw Socks poking his head out of the backpack.

"Is that a chicken?" she said.

"I'm a puppet and he's a ventriloquist," Socks said.

"Oh," the lady said, and went on.

That's when they heard tires screeching in the street as a light changed from green to red and a big gray bus slammed on its brakes so hard it seemed the driver must have been sticking his foot through the floor.

The back end of the bus lifted, and considering its size, stopped rather quickly. But it wasn't quickly enough. A car that had been going through the light properly, couldn't stop in time to avoid the front end of the bus from making impact. It smacked the car with a screech of metal and a squeal of smoking tires.

Isaac could see heads in the car right before impact.

Female driver, young kid next to her, the top of a baby's head poking up from a car seat, and then the car flipped, hit a water hydrant, sent water spraying almost as high as the four-story building next to it.

The car tumbled through a wide window display of a high-fashion clothes store. Glass rained. The car rolled inside and ended up resting on its roof. Then, due to some rare quirk of fate, burst into a roil of flames that licked out from the front end of the car and over the bottom of the chassis, cooking the tires into melting rubber in an instant. Black tire smoke billowed out of the gap in the building and swelled into the street.

Clothes and mannequins jumped ablaze and a trail of gasoline from the rear end of the car spread across the floor like an evening shadow, and the fire found it. There was a whoosh of flames, and within moments, the entire store was ablaze, mannequins melting, clothes flaming.

The driver, a young woman in a red pants suit, had been thrown free when the car made impact with the bus, right through the windshield, yet she appeared unharmed. She had been grabbed and pulled to safety by on-lookers. She kept trying to rush into the flaming store to rescue her kids, but two men held her back. The woman was screaming uncontrollably.

Isaac burst into the pawnshop, and as Buster turned to look at the sound of the bell, Isaac said, "There's trouble."

BUSTER RUSHED OUTSIDE, saw the blazing car in the clothes store, and without a word, handed his wallet to Isaac, slightly enriched with pawn shop money, and started running toward the excitement. As he ran, he felt a surge of energy and a crackling like he had been stuffed full of electricity.

A kid with a cell phone and a bad haircut started filming.

What he filmed was a portly man running toward the store, the clothes ripping off the man as he ran, green, scaly skin peeking through the rents, and in the next instant, the man had a head like a lizard and it was full of alligator teeth.

"Holy shit," said the kid, inching forward into the street, still filming with his phone.

The Lizard bounded.

It was high and fast. The bound carried him through the shattered store window, through the licking flames, where he tucked and rolled like a bowling ball fired from a catapult. He came to his feet in a flash, jumped straight toward the busted windshield through which the driver had been driven.

Glass scraped Buster's scaly hide without real damage, as he wiggled his way inside the car.

Outside, the crowd of observers, which had grown in mass, watched as Buster came out of that car, rolling again, clutching something close to him.

What the lizard was clutching was the baby seat with the baby in it.

Buster deposited the seat and squalling baby on the sidewalk, reentered the store, flames licking at him like happy dog tongues.

Isaac was at the front of the store now. He grabbed the back of the car seat and dragged it and the screaming baby down the sidewalk until she was far away from the blaze and next to her hysterical mother who quickly unfastened the restraining straps, snatched the child out of the car seat, and held the baby to her chest.

Inside the store, the flames had become even more fierce, lapping at the doors. Buster snatched an unburned red, party dress off a mannequin, peed on it, emptying a bladder as big as a gallon jug. Pulling the dress on as he ran toward the car, his tail lifting it up in back, Buster ducked his head and dove back in the car so fast it looked as if someone were throwing paint out of a bucket.

A moment later he came out with a little girl tucked under one arm. He staggered forward, into a row of smoking mannequins that toppled before him, then he tripped over them.

Buster scrambled to his feet, checked the little girl. Her hair was smoking and there were sparks in it. He used his rough, lizard hands to slap out the flames.

The flashing lights of fire trucks filled the street. Firemen jumped out of the trucks, grabbed hoses, and ran toward the fire. Amazingly, they were so focused on their jobs, they ran right past Buster, maybe thinking he was some guy in a costume, promoting something downtown.

Buster lifted the girl and sat her on one of his massive arms like she was a doll on a closet shelf.

After a moment allowing her to enjoy her perch, Buster put the little girl down gently in front of her frantic mother, and the still screaming baby she held clutched to her chest. Isaac was there too, trying to assure the mother that her children were all right. The pack with Socks in it wiggled on his back.

"What is that thing?" a woman standing nearby said.

"Monster," a man's voice yelled from the crowd. "Go back to the zoo."

Buster didn't even look up. He couldn't be loved by everyone. A giant lizard was bound to be frightening to some.

The little girl hugged her mother's leg. A paramedic bent down next to her, looking at a matted red area near her hairline where her head had banged against the glass. Her hair was singed, and she was a bit bruised, but otherwise, she was all right.

The little girl turned and looked at Buster, and he did the only thing that came to mind. He waved.

"Mommy, the big lizard saved me," the girl said.

The woman studied Buster. It was obvious she was in shock from the events, as well as there being a giant lizard in a urine-soaked, ripped, smoking, red, cocktail dress standing in front of her. "I know honey, he saved us all. Thank you, Mr...."

"I'm Bu..." Buster started, but Socks had worked the zipper loose from inside the backpack somehow, and was waving his wings like a baseball coach that didn't want him to steal third.

"They call me..." he thought a moment. "Sergeant Scales."

Buster rested his fists against his waist in a hero pose, smiled his big row of alligator teeth.

The little girl stepped forward and hugged Buster's leg.

"Thank you, Big Lizard."

"No, it's..."

The hugging continued. Buster saw the girl's sweet face looking up at him, decided it wasn't worth the trouble. A feeling he hadn't felt in a long time spread through him. A feeling he had rarely felt, in fact. It took him a moment to put the emotion together, but finally recognized what it was. Pride.

"You are welcome."

"You smell like pee," the little girl said.

"I know."

From somewhere a bottle sailed through the air and hit Buster in the back of the head, and from the crowd a voice said, "Got that cross-dressing alligator motherfucker."

BUSTER FELT GOOD ABOUT HIMSELF. It was like comic books he had read. He was a hero, big time. The bottle had been thrown by someone nervous about his reptilian appearance, but what he had done, and how the little girl made him feel special, bottle or no bottle, was a sensation he could become addicted to.

Didn't get much better than rescuing a baby and a little girl from a fire.

He was the hero.

Wearing a pee-stained cocktail dress, but a hero nonetheless.

Buster was so happy with himself he hadn't bothered to transform back into human form. As journalists arrived, and started snapping his photo, he leaped away from them, bounding along as if spring-loaded, jumping from one building to the next, scaling the walls like… well, like a lizard.

Up on the roof tops, lizard claws scuttling along so fast no one could keep up with him. He took a back-way home to the ark, though he took his time about it, learning exactly what he could do with his new-found powers. He assumed, minus the dress, he would be even more effective. He dropped from buildings, ran swiftly down alleys, the dress practically in rags. His appearance caused dogs to bark, cats to screech, and rats to scuttle into and behind garbage cans. As he ran down alleyways, homeless men and women studied him with wide eyes—having seen everything. Except for an enormous lizard in a red cocktail dress.

One of the homeless women, wrapped in an oversized flannel shirt and too-long pants tied up at the ankles with twine, wearing tennis shoes said, "That would look better with heels."

Buster ignored her.

Atop a railing that ran around the city's water tower, he disrobed, but found his lizard equipment was dangling in the wind. He used the dress to make a kind of lower body wrap, though he feared it looked like a big red diaper.

When he arrived at the ark sometime later, he was careful

not to be seen scaling the wall, dropping over to the other side.

Inside the main deck, he made his way toward a light coming from the open door to what he thought of as The Big Room. It had been an office once, and it held a long conference table, soft, but slightly molded chairs, and a long couch that he used for a bed. There was a large TV mounted on the wall, and that looked to have been something Isaac added, perhaps something he had found tossed and had brought back and fixed. That kid could fix anything but his past.

There were lots of biblical paintings on the wall. One of them, curiously, Buster noted for the first time, was a painting of Jesus with a lamb at his feet, his arm around John Wayne, who was dressed as a Centurion. In the background were more sheep on a hill where three crosses stood, the center one empty. The crosses on either side of the empty one were equipped with dangling bodies. Some smart-ass, possibly Isaac, though Socks was a better suspect, had drawn black turds dropping from one sheep's behind.

Socks, who was roosting on the table, opened his eyes, said, "Damn, you piss yourself?"

A toilet flushed, and Isaac came in from the hallway, said, "Hey, man. You were magnificent. That right there, that was some Spider-Man shit, but for real."

"It was, wasn't it," Buster said, slowly transforming, clutching the remains of the dress turned diaper, as he became smaller and it became looser.

"You know what?" Isaac said. "We should like, celebrate, get a pizza, watch a movie."

"That sounds good to me," Socks said. "I'm tired of bread. Let's go heavy on the cheese and pepperoni, put that pawn shop money to work."

"We don't have a phone to order," Buster said, having completely transformed back to human. "One second, and I'll go get us a pizza. They got some good ones at Pippo's."

"I'd recommend a shower and a change of clothes," Socks said, "or at least tie a ribbon to your dick to look festive."

Buster left the room.

Socks said, "He did do good out there, didn't he?"

"Yeah," Isaac said.

Isaac and Socks talked about the event, described what both had seen to each other, then turned to the type of pizza they should get while Buster showered.

While they waited, Isaac picked up the remote for the TV.

"Rigged all this shit up yourself, and can't get a decent cell phone?" Socks said.

"Working on it."

When the TV popped on, Isaac thought they might start with cruising Netflix for something to watch when they got the pizza. He had found a way to rig that into the system as well, but the news was on.

Buster, dressed in safari shorts, a tee-shirt and flip-flops, came into the room, glanced at the TV. There, filling the screen, was him running, transforming into Big Lizard. "Damn," he said.

"It didn't get your face before the transformation," Isaac said. "And it happened so quick, I doubt anyone really noticed what was going on before you changed."

"Look at me. I'm incredible."

"You're all right," Socks said. "Good thing you got that dress on, your whacker is hanging out."

There was footage of Buster springing through the window with first the baby, then the little girl. More footage of him standing and speaking with the mother, who he could see was nervous to be near an over-large lizard, no matter how grateful she was. He saw the bottle hit him in the back of the head. He could also clearly see the man who threw it.

"Damn," Buster said, "that was Hadrian. Last time he gets leftovers from me."

"Man," Socks said. "He's got an arm on him, and damn good aim."

There was more footage of Buster rushing along the streets, leaping from building to building, pulling the dress up over his knees with one hand, clutching the brick walls of buildings so fiercely fragments of brick rained down onto the street.

There was a lot of discussion by news folk about how amazing it all was, and who was this mystery man who could change into a lizard and wear a cocktail dress. Where did he come from? Where did he get his powers? Who was he? Was he man, woman, cross-dresser?

They interviewed the family Buster had saved, and the little girl said how much she loved Big Lizard, which made Buster happy again.

There was also the expected asshole commentator who came on to say that Big Lizard could be a menace. Who knew what he would do next?

Maybe he had rescued the children with an intent to eat them.

Stupid stuff, but his opinions were discussed as if they made sense. From the discussion, it appeared they had taken on the little girl's moniker to describe him. Big Lizard. So much for Sergeant Scales.

Eventually the news anchor moved on to other news. A camera showed a narrow street and a brownstone building, and stairs that led up the side of the building to the second-floor landing.

Buster recognized the location immediately. He felt a knot begin to form in his stomach. It was where his Aunt June lived.

A lady cop was being interviewed by a male reporter who looked as if he was playing hooky from junior high. He must have had some rich hair plaster on, as there were flies buzzing around it. The cop was pretty and tired and looked like she'd rather shoot the reporter than answer questions.

"Is it true the woman was mutilated?" the reporter asked, sticking the mic in the pretty cop's face.

"It hasn't been absolutely confirmed, but preliminary report is the woman, a Ms. June Nix, had her fingers and thumbs removed, like someone had pruned a shrub, with what we assume were garden clippers, or some similar instrument."

"Do you think this was murder?"

"No. We think she killed herself, cut all her fingers off, and then hid the weapon before she died. What the hell do they teach you in journalism school these days? They send you here from shop class by accident? What kind of stupid question was that?"

The camera went dark temporarily, then cut away to another view of the building.

"Aunt June," Buster said. "My god. It's her. She's Big Chicken's second victim."

THE WORLD WAS NEVER shiny and bright for Buster, but Aunt June had been a penlight in the darkness. She had watched after him and understood his nerdish predilections, and had encouraged him, even when he himself had lost faith. She scolded him and told him flat out what she thought was his problem without ever making it seem he was unredeemable.

She took him to the movies, and now and again to community theater, the library, museums, bookstores, and pizza parlors.

If he came over, she helped him with his homework and kept him in spending money, had even co-signed for him to buy a car when he grew into adulthood.

He had rewarded her faith in him with one failure after

another, one bad choice following on the heels of another. And now he couldn't say I'm sorry, or thank you for trying, or How About Them Mets. It was over and done.

Her funeral, a few days after her death, was in a big church downtown. The funeral had been organized by those she worked with, friends, of which she had many. Relatives, not so much. All their kin had died or wandered off somewhere to blend into the elements of the universe.

Funny thing about the church funeral, was his aunt didn't care about religion. But since it was being organized by friends and co-workers, she didn't have a say in how it was conducted. He, her only known living relative, should have been at the helm of it all. But he was no longer known to be living.

Up in the attic of the great church on Grand Street, Buster, as Big Lizard, sat quietly among the gargoyles there in the dark at the top of the cathedral, and watched the display below unfolding to the sound of sad, dark organ notes.

The service went on, music stopping intermittently for a preacher, who had never met his aunt, to sound out her virtues, all on cue cards written by admirers. What they said about her was true. Her innate goodness, and how she didn't stand for foolishness, unless it was of the fun nature, not the lazy nature, and how she had loved her nephew, who she expected great things from.

As far as anyone knew, he had fled the hospital only to die somewhere of his injuries, because no one human could survive those, not without medical treatment. It was thought one day his skull would turn up in a dog's mouth.

More music was played. The coffin was lifted from its position at the front of the church, and the pallbearers, of which he should have been one, carried it away.

As the coffin was moved, something wet fell on one of the

pallbearers. It ran out of his hair and onto his forehead, ran down his nose, fell off the tip of it, onto his upper lip.

He licked at it.

It tasted of salt. Like a tear.

The pallbearer, still carrying the coffin, glanced up.

There was nothing above but dark shadows woven between rafters, a smattering of dust, floating down, as if something had disturbed it.

In the ark, Buster, still the lizard, said, "She was killed because of her connection to me. Big Chicken is sending a message. Telling me I can't stop him, and that he is going to continue the ritual."

They were in the big meeting room, Isaac seated at the table, the chair turned toward the couch where Big Lizard sat, trying to adjust his tail comfortably. Nearby, Socks was perched on an apple crate, wings folded.

"I think we should open the book," Isaac said. "Perhaps it can help us."

"Damn," Socks said. "If we must, okay, but that book kicks me into gear, makes my gizzard rattle, connects me and my bowels with the Big Bad. I don't like going there. It makes me uncomfortable, to put it mildly."

"Have another way?" Isaac said.

Socks dipped his head, shook it a little, then looked up.

"Hell. Get me a fresh diaper and some baby wipes."

Moments later, Isaac brought out the book, opened it to a visions spell. The open book smoked green smoke and the smoke drifted up and thinned above their heads and the pages trembled.

Socks swallowed, looked straight ahead, waiting.

Nothing happened.

"Read the spell aloud," Socks said.

Isaac read the spell. They waited. Socks was obviously straining for effect, but nothing.

"Shit," Socks said. "I been out of the hole too long, I've lost my connection. I mean, I feel it, but I can't experience it."

"The hole?" Buster said.

"Yeah, the demon dimension. I've lost my juice. Hell, boys, I'm sorry."

"It's not your fault," Isaac said closing the book.

Socks clucked, said, "Okay. Here's the shit. You got to get some frayed wires with plugs on the ends. And we'll still need the book and a glass of water. After that, no matter how it turns out, I want a pizza, extra anchovies."

"Done," Buster said.

"Course, I got to hope I'm around to eat it."

THE FRAYED WIRES from two lamp cords with plugs on the ends were wrapped around each of Socks' feet. A wall socket was nearby. A glass of water was on the table.

With a fresh diaper and a determined look, Socks squatted on the table, said, "Way I figure, this will give me the jolt I need to cross back over the dimensional path and connect me with hellfire and brimstone. That sounds cool, doesn't it?"

"It does," Isaac said.

"I made it up, but I think there's something to it. The spell, and nearly dying, is how I got my brains and dimensional connections in the first place, along with something of an attitude that came with it. I think the latter comes from having been raised to be someone's lunch. Thing is, we pop the juice, along with a reading of the spell, I'll make the jump, do the hoodoo doodoo, come back with a vision or two, and I'm guessing a headache. I might also get fucking electrocuted."

"Should I read the spell first?" Isaac said.

"Think so, or I'll be barbecued before you can get it out of your mouth. Read the spell, pour a little water on my feet, then hook me up, let me have a jolt, and then unhook things. And I do mean quick."

"Gotcha," Isaac said.

"My eyes cross, or I start to shoot smoke out of my ass, be sure to pull the plugs."

"I don't know, Socks," Buster said. "This seems kind of stupid."

"What scares me," Socks said, "is you're the one to know. Okay, Isaac. A quick reading of the spell, and then fire in the hole."

Isaac poured a bit of water on Socks' feet, read the spell, and when he got close to the end, a few words left, he nodded to Buster.

Buster plugged both plugs into a wall socket, one in a top connection, one in a lower.

The electricity hit Socks like a club, knocked him off the table. He thrashed around on the floor as if doing a wild chicken boogie. They could see his bones through his feathers and skin. He batted his wings, made a squealing noise that sounded more like a banshee than a chicken.

Buster jerked the plugs free. Socks lay quivering on the floor.

"Socks," Buster said. "You all right?"

"Uh," Socks said.

"Damn," Buster said. "We should never have let him do that."

After a moment, Socks shook his head, slowly sat up.

"I'll be goddamned," Socks said. "The Mets are going to win the World Series."

"What?" Isaac said.

"What I got out of it," Socks said. "And hey, don't let me ever come up with that idea again, and let me also add I've lost my appetite for that pizza. I'm thinking something soft, mushy peas, oatmeal. Maybe some fruit juice. Oh, wait."

Socks turned rigid. "Oh my, little patterns crossing the sky. A box of fried chicken, a soaring bottle makes impact with something, a plaintive cry. A black ear in a sack, and what I think is a fried pie."

"You're hallucinating," Isaac said.

"What we're after. I'm connected with Big Chicken again. Connected with you too, Buster. Pieces of your thoughts cricket-hopped out of your head into mine. Not to mention some other thoughts and feelings from those fuckers that were in the room the night of the ritual. Got some stuff from some that are already passed through Hell's Gate and aren't coming back. All that rigmarole we went through that day, you fucking up the spell, it's given me the connections I suspected, via steady, smoking kilowatts of service that Isaac here is stealing from the electric company. Besides the Mets knowledge, which I don't think is connected, I saw stuff that's got something to do with what happens next with Big Chicken's spells. I can feel it all the way down to my some-what-burned chicken feet."

"A black ear in a sack?" Buster said.

"Yeah, I know. Shit is always pretty cryptic, isn't it? It's the way of the hoodoo. It's rarely laid out in an obvious way. Ear might belong to Mr. Potato Head. Thing is, we found out about the first killing pretty near when it was happening, the second not at all, and now we got this because I jumped in there and grabbed it."

"It was brave of you," Isaac said. "I'm like a fucking American hero."

"Could it already have happened?" Buster said. "What you saw?"

"I suppose," Socks said. "But I got this distinct tingle in my beak, a fluctuation in my liver, that tells me it hasn't. Like I said. I don't tune into the past so good. The present, the near future, I do better. But I will be betting on the Mets, though one of you will have to do it for me. Can't see me walking into a sports bar with a beak full of pawn shop money, ready to bet. I'm thinking I get more information like that, sports bets and such, maybe it'll let us finance our little endeavors."

"The senses," Buster said. "He took eyes the first time… my aunt's fingers, which means touch, so obviously the ear means sound."

"Yeah," Socks said. "That's good. Smarter than I expected. But knowing that helps us how?"

"If Big Chicken went after Buster's Aunt, I got a feeling, he's looking for anyone connected to Buster. Buster has become his nemesis. One of those things you described, Socks. A bottle hitting something. A black ear in a sack. And a box of chicken. What do they all have in common?"

Buster swished his tail. "Hadrian. I gave him the chicken to eat, and the ingrate beaned me with a bottle the other day, and he has black ears."

"Bingo," Socks said. "I think we got a winner."

LATE AFTERNOON, Buster in human form, wearing a pair of green stretch drawers under his pants, went on a hunt for Hadrian. His first thought was the pawn shop.

After becoming the topic of a news broadcast, photos of his lizard self were plastered in newspapers, the Internet, and so on; as if photos of a big lizard were necessary for identification—it wasn't like he would have to have on that red cocktail dress to be recognized. True, he might be recognized as Buster, the one who escaped the hospital, but he wasn't the kind of guy that was on everyone's mind. What he had was a lawsuit, Isaac, an angry chicken, and no past relationships closer than a payment clerk at the water office and the electric company. And mostly he had made those payments online. Now, he didn't even have that.

The kid and Socks stayed behind at the ark. The idea was they would work on trying to decipher more of the magical book, and set a kind of trap for Big Chicken. Buster was uncertain what that trap would be, but the idea of luring Big Chicken to the ark didn't set well with him. Socks thought doing it that way was best, thinking Big Chicken wouldn't expect them to set a trap in their very own hideout. Idea was to lure him there, letting him think they were unaware. Let him find out where they were without letting on it was their plan all along.

It occurred to Buster, it was likely Big Chicken, through magical designs of his own, already knew where they were.

Still, it was a plan.

Buster was thinking on all this as he neared the pawnshop and saw Hadrian come out of it.

"Hey, Hadrian," Buster said.

Hadrian turned, saw Buster. Hadrian smiled, spread his arms, said "Hey, chicken box man, how's it hanging and how are they banging?"

As Buster came closer, he said, "Hanging to the left, banging low."

"My man," Hadrian said, and stuck out a fist. Buster had never really been into colloquial greetings, as a matter of course and personal comfort, but he touched his fist to Hadrian's. Being that close, it was immediately obvious to Buster that Hadrian had been drinking. He smelled like he had been pickled.

"You been sweeping up?" Buster said.

"Naw. Came to get my pay for sweeping the other day. Don't need me but two or three times a week. Word I hear is I can make more being a sperm donor. You know, they give you a magazine and a plastic container, send you to a little room, you choke the eel until it spits in the container, give it to them, get some money. Hard cash."

"I don't know they let just anybody do that."

"If you can squeeze the sauce, you can do the job, is my take. I'm going to be checking on it."

"Good luck. I guess."

"Used to sell blood, but you get tired. Money is small and the orange juice is watery. Think it might be Tang or some such. Besides, they don't trust my blood these days. Ain't nothing wrong with me, but they don't like my looks. I mean, hell, I shower at the YMCA, wash my clothes in there too. Course, I got to wear wet clothes after that, walk around until they're dry. Not so bad in the summer, but man, dead of winter you can freeze your asshole closed. What you up to, man?"

"Out roaming about, you know. Hey, can we get a cup of coffee?"

"We'll have to share. I got to save this sweeping money for the things I need. Like a nuclear reactor I'm building."

"What?"

"Just fucking with you."

"Oh. A joke."

"Man, you're tighter than a nun's snatch. Loosen up, get some mental lube oil in you."

"Right. Let's go this way. Coffee shop on the corner."

"Hey, man, coffee is great, but would I be a turd I asked you to get me, like, you know, a scone?"

THEY AS IN THE SHOP, and as Hadrian ate his scone and sipped his coffee with the delicate touch of royalty, one pinky extended, Buster forced a grin and talked small-talk while trying to figure a way to tell Hadrian how his ears were in peril, and of course, his life.

It wasn't an easy subject to slide into. "Hadrian, do you believe in life after death?"

"Oh, shit. You ain't fixing to lay some Jesus bullshit on me, are you?"

"Let me come at it in a broader way. Do you think that there could be other areas of existence?"

"Wait, you talking about multiple dimensions, as in String Theory and so on?"

"Uh, yeah."

"Sure. Makes a lot of sense to me. You know, I think that could explain how people have had such odd beliefs about how there could be devils and demons and such. Also, I think aliens, the green ones, helped man build the pyramids with anti-gravity rays, you know, to lift the stones."

"Okay."

"Reason they can't find Bigfoot is he can switch dimensions. He's all hairy and shit, running around in the woods, and someone is closing in on him, and he splits the space-time continuum, or some such shit, with his mind, and bingo, he's in Bigfoot land. And you know what? I think there they have sightings of humans. You know, find these weird structures, and think what the fuck is this? And you know what it is?"

"Can't say that I do."

"Shopping malls from way, way, way back. And they went out of business, you see. In fact, most of humanity went out of business. And humans, the ones that survived, they've done gone to hiding in the woods and such, get seen now and then like Bigfoot gets seen here."

"Hadrian, what I'm trying to tell you, and I'm going to just go for it, and I want you to let me give you the whole scoop before you have anything to say. What I'm trying to tell you is your life may be in danger. No, *is* in danger."

Hadrian narrowed his eyes and sipped his coffee, his little finger extended. "Go on."

Buster told him the whole story, explained about Isaac and Socks, and during the telling, Hadrian listened intently. Buster ended with, "...and because we know each other a little, due to the visions from Socks—"

"The talking chicken?"

"Due to that, I believe Big Chicken—"

"Who was formerly the owner of the chicken business."

"Yes. I think he believes you and I are closer than we really are, and therefore, you're a target."

"Makes perfect sense."

"It does?" Buster said.

Hadrian nodded. "The vision is a look at the future," Hadrian said.

Buster paused and leaned back.

"Wait a second. Now I get it. The vision. I'm not preventing it. I'm helping it happen. Elroy will see us together and assume..."

Slowly, Buster turned his head and looked out the plate glass window. Across the street, standing in an alley was Elroy, wearing a long duster that covered him from neck to ankle. He had on flip-flops as well. Buster watched as Elroy turned and moved away into the shadows of the alley, stepping lively.

It occurred to Buster that he was right in his earlier musings. Elroy knew they were living in the ark. He'd found out somehow, maybe a vision spell, maybe luck, and he had been waiting to follow one of them out. More likely waiting to follow Buster, see who he met, who might be a victim Buster would care about. A fowl plan, indeed. Not a bad pun, thought Buster, he'd have to tell Socks that one.

"Man, that was that dude from them chicken commercials," Hadrian said. "Like you was saying. I seen him. Motherfucker looks taller on TV."

"Come on. I don't think he knows we saw him."

Buster didn't feel certain of that, but he was hopeful. If

Elroy saw him and Hadrian, but didn't know they had seen him, that might be a small edge.

They hurried out of the coffee shop and crossed the street. There were little feathers lying on the alley floor.

"There's one thing I left out of my story," Buster said.

"Being?"

"You know that big lizard you hit in the back of the head with a bottle?"

"Yeah."

"That's me."

"Ah, now, hell. Really?"

"Really."

"Now we're getting into the unbelievable shit. Damn. You're the lizard, I got to tell you, I've had the creepy crawlies since I was a kid about reptiles. My sister used to catch them and throw them on me. Damn lizard's just a step up from a fucking snake. The legs make them higher on the scale. That was a little joke there. Scale."

"Yeah. I got it."

To convince Hadrian that he was on the level, Buster transformed into Big Lizard in the recesses of the alley.

"Holy shit," Hadrian said. "How the fuck can that be?"

"It's a long story, but it has to do with dimensional magic or some such shit, stuff you were talking about, maybe some of that string theory business."

"Goddamn, man. Don't eat my ass, okay."

Big Lizard swished his tail. "One suggestion for future engagement. Don't throw bottles at me."

"That's a big ten-four."

Buster filled Hadrian in with the whole five senses thing, and how Hadrian was next on the list. When he finished the nutshell version, Hadrian wrinkled his brows.

"That's some heavy stuff, man."

"Ain't it. I want you to get on my back."

"Something about that don't sound right."

"We're going to cover some ground. Put your arms around my neck, and hang on for dear life."

Hadrian reluctantly wrapped his legs around Big Lizard's body, his arms around his neck. Big Lizard started up the alley wall effortlessly. "Aw, fuck me," Hadrian said.

Big Lizard leaped from one roof to the next, scrambled down walls and bolted through alleys. It was broad daylight, so he didn't go unnoticed. People stuck their heads out of windows and looked around the corners of alleys, pointed and chattered. Big Lizard decided to dart into the creek bed, make his way more stealthily to the ark.

Hadrian clung for dear life.

WHEN THEY ARRIVED at the ark, Big Lizard scuttled up the wall with Hadrian still desperately clinging. He lighted down on the runway that ran around the edge of the ark.

Buster waited for Hadrian to let go and climb off his back.

"You gonna get down?"

"Sorry, Lizard Guy. I've had my eyes closed last couple blocks," Hadrian said. "Didn't know we had come to a stop. I'm going to be honest. I got a hard on."

"Don't mention that again."

Hadrian dropped onto the deck, a little wobbly, stepping around like an infant taking its first steps.

"You alright there?" Buster said.

"Just trying to get my sea legs," Hadrian said. "Get it? 'Cause of the boat? The ark?"

"I get it."

Buster peered over the side of the ark, wondering if Big Chicken had followed them. What kind of mobility did a giant chicken have? The red convertible? A fucking gyrocopter?

Hadrian peered out as well. "Can he fly?"

"Real chickens can't fly," Buster said. "They can glide a little."

"I know that," Hadrian said. "I just don't know the rules when it comes to demonic shapeshifting man-chickens like you were telling me about."

"I don't think he can," Buster said.

"You don't think?"

"I hadn't thought about it. He might be able to shoot lasers from his eyes for all I know. Crap dynamite. I'm mostly working in the dark here."

They ventured forward. As they approached the Noah robot, it spoke. "TWO BY TWO."

"Fuck you," Big Lizard said. "You're in a mood."

As they walked, Buster began to shift from his lizard form. As they came to the doors, they opened, and Isaac was standing there.

"Glad you found him," Isaac said. "I got this place rigged up. Come in and I'll show you the new setup. Hey, man."

"Hey to you too," Hadrian said. "Seen you around. I always feared this place. Saw lights a few times, heard things. Thought it was ghosts."

Inside, Buster shut the doors and threw the latch.

"What do you think," Isaac said.

"About what?"

"Exactly," Isaac said. "Socks, hit the lights."

There was a whine from the generator and a sudden brightness. Buster could see now that the floor was painted with a pentagram, a big one, maybe ten feet in diameter. Bright red pentagram inside a yellow circle. The tiles under the pentagram were each decorated with little animals in pairs. Buster couldn't decide if one of the tiles represented two kangaroos, or a couple of mice.

"Colors of power," Isaac said. "Blood red, sunlight yellow. The cute little animal tiles come free."

Socks came out of the shadows near the back of the ark. He was carrying a rag between his wings, wiping his feather tips. He had spats and smears of grease on his white plumage. "That generator is one nasty fucking piece of work."

"Holy shit, a talking chicken with an eye patch," Hadrian said. "And he's a hen and sounds like a man. That just isn't right."

"Get used to it," Socks said. "After meeting you, Hadrian, I'm thinking, Buster, you ought to take your homeless guy and carry him back to his damp cardboard box, give him a box of crackers and wish him good luck."

"I could eat a cracker," Hadrian said. "But that's not fair, man. I don't have no cardboard box. I'm between habitations."

"Yeah, and where I come from my kind usually end up between a biscuit and a side of mashed potatoes, coleslaw optional, so pardon me if I don't weep for your ragged, rain-swept ass."

"Let it go, guys," Buster said.

"Thing is, me and Socks, we got a little surprise for Big Chicken, once we get him inside the pentagram," Isaac said. "We call it the anti-Big-Chicken defense."

"Yeah," Socks said, dropping the greasy rag on the floor. "We're going to read a containment spell, which may or may not work, being as we're dealing with a chicken of large size, not a demon for which it's devised. But if it works, if the pentagram holds him, then we got another surprise. Let me show you. Y'all move back about six feet."

Buster and Hadrian did just that. "Hit it, Isaac," Socks said.

Isaac, standing well out of the pentagram, picked up a bulky block with a large cable running from it into the wall. There was a switch on the block. He touched the switch.

Charging out of the darkness on a railing came a robotic

woman. She was stocky and held her rubbery hands out toward them. There was a long iron rod with a sharpened end at the tip of it. The spear extended well into the pentagram, and then Isaac hit another switch, and suddenly the rod glowed bright blue and sparkled with crackling electricity.

From the robot came Socks' recorded voice. "Hachachacha."

"That'll light him up," Isaac said.

"Damn," Hadrian said. "That's some mean shit."

"Not mean enough in my view," Socks said. "First, we got to lure him in. Then we got to have him stand in an exact spot inside the circle. The iron rod has to punch into him, and the electricity has to give him the sparkle. Then Isaac has to get the gasoline on him. Electricity ought to make him catch fire. But here's some hold-ups, Buster. You got to get him in the circle and close enough for the rod to punch him, because we only got so much track to run Mrs. Noah on. Guess that's who it is. Couldn't figure who else it could be, maybe one of the wives of one of Noah's sons. A stowaway. Not sure. Originally, she was holding a plate with roast duck on it, head and all. I guess they must have brought a few extra ducks when they loaded the ark. Anyway, we replaced the plate and duck with that spear."

"The spell is the problem and the solution," Isaac said. "You get Big Chicken in the circle, I finish the spell Socks helped translate, and he's trapped. But the kicker is, so are you Buster. We got to hope we kill him so we can break the spell and let you out. And another bummer is the spell doesn't last all that long."

"Can't we get him in the circle, then I step out, and you finish the spell?" Buster said.

"I think you'll be a little busy to manage that," Socks said. "Homeless guy here—"

"Hey," Hadrian said.

"Excuse me all to hell," Socks said. "What chateau are you living in?"

"Yeah. Okay. You got me there."

"Homeless guy here is the lure, and so are all of us. Two dead already, he's got with us one spare. He can't make the spell work if he kills us all at once, but he probably would love to capture the rest of us, and wait our turn until he takes the body part he needs. That would be his thing, Buster. All your friends. And one spare. I think maybe Hadrian is actually the spare."

"Hey," Hadrian said. "I don't mind waiting."

"The spare can die at any time," Socks said.

"Oh," Hadrian said.

"Thing is," Socks said, "we got it all planned, and it's great if we fool him into coming in here so we can do what me and Isaac have planned. Fire cleanses evil it's said, and if that's true, we're fucking golden. But, man, that's all a lot of ifs."

"Any better ideas?" Buster said.

"Not from us," Socks said.

"Okay, then," Buster said. "We got what we got."

"That don't sound so reassuring," Hadrian said.

"Goddamn it," Socks said.

Socks had managed to find a pair of cheater glasses in a drawer in a room inside the ark, and had succeeded in hooking those on his head with a strap. He was reading the local paper, as he had become quite dexterous with his wing tips.

"That motherfucker outsmarted us, and I didn't get any juice from it, no pre-warning, not even an aftermath symbolic reach-around."

They were all in the study, kicking back. Hadrian was asleep on the couch, but Socks' outburst had stirred him.

"He claimed his third victim last night. He took a tongue for taste. We were so damn certain he was after us, and maybe he knew we thought that. Whatever, he got some guy riding on a bicycle. Says here an enormous chicken in a red convertible ran over the guy, then backed over him, and then when bystanders tried to stop him, he threw them in a ditch. Bones were broken. Pride was shattered, and while they were moaning and groaning, Big Chicken pulled the tongue out of the dead bicycler's mouth. Listen here.

"One bystander said, 'Damn big ole chicken just pulled his tongue out like he was jerking a paper towel out of a bathroom dispenser. Blood went everywhere.'"

"Shit," Hadrian said. "Now I can be certain you guys ain't full of shit. How safe are we here?"

"Marginal," Isaac said, shutting off the television.

"Not what I wanted to hear."

"You know," Buster said, "I think he's trying to lure us out, have us make a mistake."

"Already made one," Socks said. "We sat here doodling our doodles, waiting on him, got all them security cameras set up, trip wire lights to let us know he's in the ark, and he runs over some guy on a bicycle. Ruined the bicycle too. Say it's beyond repair. One of those good mountain bikes."

"I think we don't have a choice," Buster said. "He may not like us very much, but the thing is, he finishes the ritual, then he's set for another five years."

"But he won't be Big Chicken anymore," Socks said. "Least I don't think so. We could get him then."

"But two more will die," Isaac said.

"Yeah, but it might not be any of us."

"No. We can't wait him out. That would be chicken."

"Watch it," Socks said. "We have to go after him."

"I think he'd win," Isaac said. "No disrespect to you, Buster, any of us, but he got more chicken than you got lizard. Something like that."

"Still, we can't just wait it out."

"I could," Hadrian said.

"Me too," Socks said. "Better two others than one of me."

"Do what you must," Buster said. "I'm going to get him."

"I'm in," Isaac said.

There was a long moment of silence.

"Ah, shit," Socks said. "I'm in, with an opportunity to change my mind later."

"I got to think about it," Hadrian said. "I like the comfort of this couch, got a toilet that flushes, and found some jerk-off magazines in the back room."

"Those are agriculture magazines," Socks said.

"Really," Hadrian said. "Look here. I ain't going. I want to die without going right at it, know what I mean. I'm safer here. Tell you the truth, I got my exit dreams. Know what I'm saying? I die, I'd like a Viking funeral."

"Yeah?" Socks said.

"Yep. With a twist. I don't want no damn boat, but put me in a sports car, set me behind the wheel and point me toward the old gravel quarry outside of town. Quarry is done, and it's full of water now, and when the sun sets out there on it, it's mighty fine and mighty red. Just set my ass on fire, and pop the gear and send me out into the quarry at top speed. That's the way to go, far as I'm concerned. After I'm dead, of course."

"Yeah," Socks said. "I got a feeling that shit ain't happening."

THE SHACK WAS EMPTY.

Buster and Isaac and Socks had concluded that Big Chicken had to be hiding someplace he knew from before, some place comfortable. First, they tried his home, which was easy to locate, and was an obvious choice, but nothing.

The grass was grown up and there were piles of Tiktaalik newspapers on the porch. He had abandoned his old world altogether, it seemed.

But their second pick, the shack on the Pick-A-Chicken property showed signs of recent habitation. There were pot pie boxes in the trash can next to the microwave, and there were empty cans of soda in the trash as well. Packs of sunflower seeds. He had left a cigarette lighter on the table with his father's name on it. It was gold and scratched from long use.

Isaac picked up the lighter. "We might find a use for this."

"I been wanting a cigar," Socks said.

"Not in my ark," Isaac said, but he pocketed the lighter.

"We could set up a trap here," Isaac said.

"Yeah," Buster said. "But we'll need a few things, and it'll have to be a different setup than the one in the ark. No lady with a spear. But we could fix up that pentagram on the floor, maybe douse him in flames, say the spell. Get it all set up, then hide and wait for him to come back. It's a crap shoot, but at this point, what isn't? What do you think?"

"What the shit," Socks said. "Might as well. Let's head back and get the stuff before Hadrian burns the place down or steals us blind, leaves a pile of shit in the board room."

"I don't think Hadrian's like that," Buster said.

NIGHT WAS FALLING as they made their way back to the ark, Buster transforming to lizard, his green short, stretch pants expanding with him. Isaac climbed on Buster's back, Socks perched on Isaac's shoulder, his talons deep in the old worn jacket Isaac was wearing. And away they went, Buster leaping away, the two of them clinging.

They used a secret pass-way that Isaac had a key for, door behind a clutch of shrubs that grew near the wall. It had been used for deliveries when the ark was a functional park and the shrubs less wild.

As they walked along, Buster changed back to his original form. The stretch shorts still fit. They were a great costume. Flexible, yet they would go back to their original size with ease.

They climbed the stairs to the second level. Noah greeted them and recommended two by two. As they opened the double doors, and entered, the doors slid closed behind them, and the lights came on.

Standing to their right was Big Chicken, his wing tip on the light switch. He had Hadrian's ears strung through a string that was hung around his neck.

"Surprise, motherfuckers," Big Chicken said.

And there they were standing in the circle containing the pentagram. There was a grating sound, and Noah's wife came forward with her spear. Dangling from it was Hadrian, feet just off the floor. He was alive, but his skin was the color of cigarette ash. Where his ears had been there was much blood, and it ran down his cheeks and over his shoulders and dripped on the floor.

"Your friend here was talkative," Big Chicken said. "When I got here, he was putting goods in a gunny sack. He was going to rob you."

Hadrian tried to lift his head, but it might as well have been a bag of bricks. He couldn't do it. Blood dribbled from his mouth.

"He may be a thief, but he's our thief," Socks said.

"He told me what kind of plans you had for me, but hey, I've beat you to the punch."

"Let us get him off of that thing."

"Oh, I wouldn't bother. Vital organs were punctured. Besides, it's pointless. I'm about to kill every jerk-wad one of you. And then I'm going to cook you, little hen."

"You horrid sonofabitch," Buster said. There was a crackling noise, like someone wadding up aluminum foil, and he began to transform again.

"Nice outfit," Big Chicken said.

Big Lizard sprang over the pentagram with a growl. He and Big Chicken came together like colliding train engines, rolled across the floor and into the den. Punches were exchanged. Beaks punctured green flesh. Fangs bit. Feathers flew.

Socks fluttered through the door, kind of skip-jumping, wings beating. "Step-over toe hold, Buster. Step-over toe hold."

Isaac tried to gently pull Hadrian off the spear. Hadrian made a gurgling noise, lifted his hand and touched Isaac's. He managed to shake his head slightly. "No use," he said, then grabbed a deep breath, wriggled on the spear, and went still.

"So, sorry, Hadrian," Isaac said.

MEANWHILE, back in the board room...

The room was full of blood and feathers and shreds of scales. Both Big Chicken and Big Lizard had gained their feet, and it was a slug fest. It sounded like someone beating a Naugahyde couch with a belt in there. Big Lizard and Big Chicken took shots hard enough to rattle a gorilla's bones, but neither went down.

The animals in cages jumped up as they passed the sensors and Noah could be heard saying, "TWO BY TWO" as the battle raged on.

Socks was hopping up and down, offering esoteric wrestling advice, which Big Lizard was ignoring, and probably didn't understand.

"Pile driver," Socks repeated again and again.

Isaac rushed into the room. He had the spell book. He opened it.

"We need them in the pentagram, kid," Socks said.

"Hold the book."

Isaac handed it to Socks, and though Socks took it, the weight was too much for his wings, and it drove him and his wing-tips to the ground. Isaac charged past the fighters, and disappeared into a back room. After a bit, Isaac came riding in on the garden tractor, pushed it into Big Chicken's ass. This drove the Chicken forward, and gave Buster a break. Buster hit him with an uppercut that nearly caused Big Chicken to attain moon orbit.

And then, what goes up, must come down. Down goes Big Chicken.

Up comes Big Chicken. He turned and grabbed the little garden tractor, picked it up as if it were a cardboard box, and sent Isaac tumbling. He lifted it to throw at Isaac, who was on his back, scuttling with his hands and knees like a crab, trying to get away.

Big Lizard tackled Big Chicken, sending the tractor scooting over the floor. Socks, minus the book, leaped, landed on Big Chicken's head, bent forward and beaked out Big Chicken's eye. It came out with a gush of blood and spurt of goo and a string of tendons. Big Chicken let out with a sound somewhere between a scream and a squawk.

"My eye!" Big Chicken yelled. "My eye!"

"Got it right here," Socks said, now on the floor, standing on one leg, lifting the other leg, the talon of which held the blood-dripping eyeball he had transferred from his beak. Blood covered Big Chicken's face. Socks had dealt a real blow.

"Now we're even," Socks said.

Socks used his back leg to lift the eyeball to his beak, and gobbled at it, snapping it to pieces, chewing it and swallowing it in a dramatic show.

"You fucking chicken cunt. I'll cook you alive in boiling oil," Big Chicken said.

While he was distracted, Big Lizard tackled him.

A rolling ball of lizard and chicken tumbled through the door between the board room and the front room, and Big Lizard managed to roll them into the pentagram.

Isaac staggering to his feet, took hold of the book again. He flipped it open, started reading the spell aloud. Big Chicken had opened a real can of whup-ass. He had Big Lizard by the tail and was lifting him up and slamming him down, as easily as if Big Lizard were a fly-swatter.

"Ugh. Shit. Goddamn. Fuck," Big Lizard said. Isaac continued reading the spell. The air shimmered and glowed lightly around the circle containing the pentagram. When Isaac finished the spell, he said, "He's trapped. You got this."

"I don't think so," Big Lizard said as he was lifted as light as a fart on a high wind, and flung against the force shield around the pentagram.

As Big Lizard hit the invisible barrier, a tooth came out of his mouth and rattled on the floor. Big Lizard slid down the invisible wall like a gooey booger on hot glass.

"He's getting whipped like a rented mule," Socks said, flapping over next to Isaac.

"He'll take him," Isaac said.

"Take him where? Big Chicken beats him any harder, we'll be able to slide him through a crack under a door."

Big Lizard was up now, running around and around the pentagram with Big Chicken in pursuit.

Big Lizard wheeled suddenly, leaped with both feet out, kicked Big Chicken backwards, against the magic barrier. It was a good blow. Big Chicken tried to get up. Big Lizard was on him like a pig on truffles, started slinging knuckles, pounding Big Chicken's head with hard, loud shots.

"Wake up, kid," Socks said. "Grab the cable."

Isaac broke from his stupor, wheeled and grabbed the prepared cable. Socks touched a wing-tip to the switch, waited.

Standing at the edge of the circle, cable in hand, Isaac saw that Big Chicken had taken the lead. He had found his feet and tripped Big Lizard with a sweep of his foot. When Big Lizard slammed to his back, Big Chicken straddled him and began knocking knots on Big Lizard's scaly head faster than a computer could count them.

Isaac waited for when they would separate, but it didn't seem to come.

Socks said, "They can't go out, but the spell don't keep someone from going in. You're gonna have to work the switch yourself, kid."

Socks grabbed at his feathery sides, as if hitching up his pants, tugged, and then flapped his wings enough to sail into the enchanted circle. He landed on Big Chicken's head, beating his wings, clawing with his talons.

He bent forward and pecked at Big Chicken's other eye, but missed. Big Chicken grabbed him and sent him sailing, crashing into the barrier like a racquet ball. Socks slid down it, said, "Ouch."

That was Big Lizard's moment, he rolled Big Chicken off of him, rolled him in such a way he managed to kick Big Chicken a solid one in the stomach. As the two came apart, springing to their feet, Isaac hit the switch and poked the cable across the barrier. When he touched it to the back of Big Chicken's head, the fowl lit up like Las Vegas on a Friday night.

It made Big Chicken dance, made his bones light up. You could see his organs swimming around in there.

Buster snatched the extended cable from Isaac, said, "Gas and spell, Isaac."

Big Lizard jammed the cable into Big Chicken again. More dance moves occurred and Big Chicken smoked and finally fell in a heap. Isaac slid the gas can into the circle.

Big Lizard tossed the cable aside, grabbed the can and splashed his collapsed foe with gasoline.

Even after all that, Big Chicken was trying to get up. Buster swung the can and knocked him to the edge of the circle, and that's when Isaac popped open the lighter he had taken from the shack. He thumbed a flame, flipped the lit lighter onto the gas-damp chicken. When he did, fire leaped alive, and the heat was blistering. The air smelled of ozone and chicken shit.

Big Chicken began to run around the circle wildly, blazing like the Olympic torch. As he ran, Big Lizard extended a foot and tripped him.

Isaac began to read the finishing spell.

The flaming chicken, face down, feathers smoking, burned with a crispy sound, and then a black cloud of smoke formed over him. The cloud turned into the shape of a large chicken, swirled in the smoke and took on the shape of a human being. One eye burned like a lit cigarette tip, then the blazing eye and hazy shape, whirled into a little tornado and rose, spun momentarily, then dipped and went straight through the floor without leaving a mark.

There was only the muffled sound of Big Chicken/Elroy's last word.

"Charlotte."

Isaac continued to read the finishing spell.

The air became as still and heavy as a fresco on stone. The air smelled of fried chicken and eternal damnation.

Just for a moment, the inside of the pentagram flashed orange and red and an abyss of deep fire could be seen, and Elroy, no longer a chicken, was tumbling into it. His screams were loud and strained enough to make the skin on a mule's dick roll back. Then the image snapped away, leaving only Isaac, and Buster, the still, little shape of Socks, and the speared, blood-dripping body of Hadrian, dangling from Mrs. Noah's spear.

🦃

When the spell of the pentagram was broken, Big Lizard transformed, his corpulent body snug in the shrunken short pants. He hurried over to Socks, Isaac coming in the circle as well.

"Socks, for god sakes, Socks," Buster said, shaking the little chicken.

One of Socks' legs kicked a little. He opened his one eye. "Anyone get the number of that truck?"

Buster sighed, relieved. "Is he dead?" Socks said.

"More than dead," Isaac said, coming into the circle, bending down next to Socks. "He's gone to where he deserves. He didn't finish the bargain, and Buster here gave him an ass whipping."

"That's the story I'm telling if anyone asks," Buster said. "Isaac here finished him off. And that was a brave thing you did, Socks."

"I know," Socks said.

"I thought I heard Big Chicken say something, at the end."

"I think he said car lot," Buster said.

Later that day, they discovered Big Chicken's convertible parked along the creek bank in a picnic area. The keys were under the floor mat. Buster drove it to the ark, Socks and Isaac in the backseat.

They drove the convertible inside through the double-wide doors. They put Hadrian in the trunk along with a can of gasoline and a concrete block left over from ark construction, drove out to the quarry Hadrian had mentioned. It was nearly sunset.

Buster and Isaac put Hadrian behind the wheel, poured gasoline over him, started the engine, let it idle with the gear in park. They put the concrete block on the gas pedal. The car roared like a lion. Buster changed into Big Lizard, climbed in on the front passenger side. "Light it up," he said.

Isaac thumbed the lighter to life, tossed it onto Hadrian as Buster pulled the gear into drive. The flames jumped and Buster jerked back against the passenger door. Then, light as a feather, flipped backwards over the side and landed on his feet, just in time to see Hadrian, flaming like a Viking chieftain, go over the lip of the quarry as sunset dropped orange and yellow over the rocks and trees. The car and its passenger sailed way out and down into the deep water with a loud splash.

When they gathered at the edge of the quarry, and looked at the water, it was rippling and there was a faint sight of smoke trailing over the surface. The rear end of the red convertible was faintly visible, then gone.

Night seeped in through the trees and fell down on them like a concrete shadow.

Isaac climbed on Buster's back. Socks climbed on Isaac's shoulder, burying his talons into the rough jacket.

Big Lizard, started to run, and finally he began to leap. The leaps were long and smooth, and he could see well in the dark when he was transformed, and he saw the world anew, and fresh. Buster felt comfortable bounding through the dark in his new and powerful skin.

The skin of a hero.

ABOUT THE AUTHORS

Joe R. Lansdale is the author of over fifty novels and four hundred shorter works, including stories, essays, reviews, film and TV scripts, introductions and magazine articles. His work has been made into films (*Bubba Ho-Tep*, *Cold in July*, & *The thicket*, as well as the acclaimed TV series, *Hap and Leonard*). He has also had works adapted to *Masters of Horror* on Showtime, and wrote scripts for *Batman: The Animated Series*, and *Superman: The Animated Series*. He scripted a special Jonah Hex animated short, as well as the animated Batman film, *Son of Batman*. He has also written scripts for John Irvin, John Wells, and Ridley Scott.

He has received numerous recognitions for his work. Among them the Edgar, for his crime novel *The Bottoms*, the Spur, for his historical western *Paradise Sky*, as well as ten Bram Stokers for his horror works. He has also received the Grand Master Award and the Lifetime Achievement Award from the Horror Writers Association. He has been recognized for his contributions to comics with the Inkpot Life Achievement Award, and has received the British Fantasy Award, and has had two *New York Times* Notable Books. He has been honored with the Italian Grinzane Cavour Prize, the Sugar Pulp Prize for fiction, and the Raymond Chandler Lifetime Achievement Award. *Edge of Dark Water* was listed by *Booklist* as an Editor's Choice, and the American Library Association chose *The Thicket*, for Adult Books for Young Adults. *Library Journal* voted *The Thicket*, as one of the Best Historical Novels of the Year.

He has also received an American Mystery Award, the Horror Critics Award, and the Shot in the Dark International Crime Writer's Award. He was recognized for his contributions to the legacy of Edgar Rice Burroughs with the Golden Lion Award. He is a member of the Texas Institute of Literature and has been inducted into the Texas Literary Hall of Fame and is Writer in Residence at Stephen F. Austin State University.

His work has also been nominated multiple times for the World Fantasy Award, the Bram Stoker Awards, the Macavity Award, the Dashiell Hammett Award, and others.

He has been inducted into the International Martial Arts Hall of Fame, as well as the United States Martial Arts Hall of Fame and is the founder of the Shen Chuan martial arts system.

His books and stories have been translated into many languages.

He lives in Nacogdoches, Texas with his wife, Karen, their pit-bull, and a cranky cat.

Keith Lansdale has adapted and written multiple scripts for film such as *The Projectionist* (currently in pre-production), *The Promise, Best Sellers Guaranteed, The Weight,* and *The Pale Door. Christmas with the Dead* was previously filmed in 2012 and has recently been readapted to be filmed again with Lansdale directing the project. It has also been adapted for a stage musical.

Keith has adapted multiple comics such as *Hoot Goes There?,* a short *X-Files* series for IDW comics, the short story "Mud" for *Creepy,* and *Prisoner of Violence* (an extension of the *Prisoner 489* universe by Joe R. Lansdale), along with comic adaptations of *Crawling Sky* for Antarctic Press, *Vampirella* for Diamond comics, *Dog, Cat, and Baby* for Dark Horse and Avatar comics, as well as *God of the Razor,* "The Dump," and "The Fat Man" for other comic companies. Most recently he has picked up the mantle of Joe R. Lansdale's *Red Range,* with *Red Range: Pirates of Fireworld* now headed to print.

Keith also co-wrote the children's short story "The Companion" when he was twelve with his younger sister which was picked up by *Creepshow,* and was co-author of *In Waders from Mars* at the age of four. He was also a co-editor for *Son of Retro Pulp Tales,* published by Subterranean Press.